JESUS CHRISTS

a novel

A.J. LANGGUTH

JESUS CHRISTS
By A.J. Langguth

Published by
FIGUEROA PRESS
Suite 401E
840 Childs Way
Los Angeles, CA 90089
(213) 740-3570
(213) 740-5203
www.figueroapress.com

Figueroa Press is a division of the USC University Bookstore

Cover design by Jeff Ratto, USC Graphic Design

Cimabue Crucifix fragment credit: David Lees/Timepix

Produced by Crestec Los Angeles, Inc.

Printed in the United States of America

Published in 1968 by Harper & Row, 1969 by Ballantine Books

LIBRARY OF CONGRESS CATALOGUING-IN-PUBLICATION DATA
Langguth, A.J.
Jesus Christs
Includes no bibliographical references (p.) or index
ISBN: 0-9727625-0-7
LCN: 2003103242

JESUS CHRISTS

Los Angeles, California

"I HAVE come to die for your sins," Jesus told a stooped figure passing him on the road.

"Then what am I to die for?" the old man asked.

Jesus took a small notebook from his pocket and copied the question. "If I may have your name and address," he said, "an answer will be sent to you."

Most miracles passed unrecorded. Once, when Jesus was apart from his disciples for an afternoon, he waved a hand and turned all the desert brush and flowers white. Curious at his

1

powers, he waved again. But there was no change, and the colors did not return.

Jesus sank then to his knees to ask how he had offended God. The answer came at last: Only his touch would restore life. Rising, Jesus began with the bush nearest him. Under his hand, green flowed from the roots and spread through the branches. He passed across the desert floor, touching each sprig and leaf, until the scene was as fresh as when he had come upon it.

That was my lesson for today, he told himself as he went to rejoin his disciples, and it was not a solemn one.

He was both: a prisoner about to be strapped into the electric chair and a chaplain who had come to comfort him. They recognized each other at once, but the captive Jesus sensed some antagonism from the Jesus priest. "What's the matter?" He spoke quietly enough that the warden and guards could not overhear. "I'm the one who's going to fry. Why should you look so grim?"

"I'd expected to be finished by this time. The demands on me have been almost more than I can stand. It's not fair that you should be released first."

The prisoner took the priest's hand. Let the guards think he was pleading for mercy. "God must think they need a priest in their midst more than a traitor. We don't have to agree."

"Don't smile. It looks odd. And don't expect sympathy about the treason. Next year everybody will know you did the right thing."

"What will they be saying about you next year?"

"That I was afraid."

"I was afraid until today. How will you get it?"

"I hope this way. It's supposed to be quick."

"I'll let you know." The prisoner pointed to the men in the corridor. "They're looking eager." He released the priest's wet hand. "Thanks for stopping by."

"It helped me."

A guard had entered the cell and stood between them. "Isn't that what these talks are for?" the prisoner intoned. "To ease the mind and soothe the troubled spirit?"

"He's been like that the whole time, Father," the guard said apologetically to the priest. "He doesn't take anything seriously."

Against all odds, they found themselves in the same place some years later. This time it was the priest who was awaiting electrocution, and he was much merrier.

"Of course I remember you," the other Jesus said. "You had a long face that morning and a homely one."

"I was worried then about not being able to recognize Judas. That seems foolish to me now. Have you ever had trouble knowing which one he was?"

"Never. He's usually the foreman on my jury."

"He was my archbishop."

"I remember the one. He's being canonized."

"They say he was a good man except for what he did to me."

"The warden is motioning for me to bring you out."

"I'm ready."

"You're getting what you wanted."

"Too late."

"That's the joke, isn't it? You always get it, and it's always too late."

"Is that supposed to cheer me up?"

"It can still make me laugh," the visiting Jesus said.

Moans were still drifting up from the bottom of the precipice when the black prince ordered Jesus brought to his tent.

"I have killed two hundred men today, my little pet," the prince began softly. He sank to his knees and kissed Jesus' fettered hands. "Why do I do these things? Tell me! I love my people. Why do I kill them? I ripped into one old man with my own sword. Here it is." He drew the blade, rusting with blood, from its gold scabbard. "You see? I am not afraid to kill. I am not afraid of your God. He is nothing to me. When I see him at last, I will smite his eyes and cut out his lying tongue.

"Oh, little pet! Make me stop! He is my God, too, and I adore him. I ordered them, men and children, thrown over the cliff—ten, fifteen, twenty men, pleading and weeping as I gave the orders." He laughed and showed his strong white teeth. "But all those men did not die. Some of them are alive down there. Do you hear them? My aides say they will last until morning. I want to hear their screams as I go to sleep. Their cries will lull me."

Jesus said, "I must go back to the others."

"You will go back when I permit it, missionary." The prince reached out to embrace Jesus by the waist. "Oh, my pet, if only I could have you forever with me, perhaps I would not commit these crimes. But too often I must be gone, and you must stay here."

"In your prison."

"In my prison, because otherwise you would leave me and I would die without you. We are one man, you and I. How often have I felt as you spoke that I was watching and listening to myself. But you would not kill like this, would you? So we are not the same."

"I have never understood killing," Jesus answered. "It must

be a failing in me, for other men think highly of it."

"It is beautiful. I took my sword, this sword, and put the tip against his chest and hardly pushed at all. One minute he was a venerable old man, old enough to be my grandfather. The next instant he was a crumpled bag of garbage. I did that. I took his life from him, and I felt his life join with mine and make me stronger. Why don't you congratulate me? Don't you want to see me strong?"

"That is not strength. There is only one strength and it does not come from killing."

The prince sprawled indolently across his silken couch. "Tell me about strength."

"We have spoken of it many times. You need no instruction from me."

"I have learned from you everything that you have to teach? If you say that, you have not studied the literature of our world. You have been in Magdala barely three hundred nights. Your God should have given you three times as many stories to tell. But I have loved you while you were here. You are a finer man than I could ever be. I will be glad to be rid of you."

The prince called to his guard and gestured toward Jesus. "I will weep for you," he said, as the soldier seized Jesus and moved him toward the cliff. "No, I will weep for myself and for what you have forced me to do to you."

The soldier thrust Jesus over the edge, and the prince drew close to listen for any new note among the groaning and cries from below. When he could hear none, he ordered the guard to go down and investigate.

"Would he be lying there alive but refusing to moan?" the prince asked aloud as he awaited a report. "Would he try to spite me by denying me the sound of his suffering?"

"He is dead, Your Highness." The guard's face was flaked with dirt from his climb on the cliff.

"I knew he would not toy with me. I will miss him more than I can say. Guard?"

"Yes, Your Highness?"

"Remind me that if he comes again, we must torture him before we kill him."

"I will remember, Your Highness."

"Or should I let him torture me? What do you think, guard? Which would you like better?"

"I have no opinion, Your Highness."

The prince threw himself again on his couch and buried his face in his pale palms. "You're right. It doesn't matter. Either way it is the same. I want him back! Are you listening to me, guard? I want him back!"

"He is dead, Your Highness."

"No! I am dead, and he is living. Does that surprise you, guard? I am dead. I was killed when you pushed him off that cliff. You are too stupid to understand. He would understand."

The guard watched with pleasure as tears ran down the prince's smooth cheeks. "He is dead, Your Highness," he repeated distinctly. "He is dead."

Nathanael was seventeen years old, a fact Jesus tried to bear in mind. "Jesus! Jesus!" he cried as he burst into the study.

"Yes?"

"If you came to die for men's sins—"

"The word you want is 'since.' "

"Since you came to die for men's sins—"

"Yes?"

"Shouldn't you have said, 'Forgive me, Father, for what they are about to do'?"

"Is that all, Nathanael?"

"I thought of it while I was walking to the bus stop. I ran all the way back."

"Close the door firmly on your way out, will you, please?"

"Yes, sir."

"Carefully!" he warned them in a weak voice. "Don't drop me."

A stone turned under James's foot. "Quiet!" Christ whispered. "Can't you be quiet? We'll have the whole regiment back here."

They laid him gently by the mouth of the cave. James said, "I don't feel much like wrestling with that stone again."

"It would be awfully nice—" this came from Thomas—"if someone we knew would consider it a good time for a miracle and let some angel swing the rock back."

Christ grunted. "Get to work. It's not heavy. But quietly."

"Far be it from me to complain," Thomas drawled, "but I've been around a long time, and I've never seen one of those miracles we all hear so much about. Did any of you actually talk to Lazarus after his amazing recovery?"

Christ smiled with the others. "You've missed nothing, Thomas. You wouldn't have found him lively at any time."

Thomas was distinguished for his round belly, quivering big nose and nearsighted squint. He was a man counted in because he would have been so wretched if he had been left out.

When they were alone, Peter said to Jesus, "You have the whole of tomorrow ahead of you. Have you decided how to spend it?"

"I would like to be alone. Afterward there may not be much chance."

"Of the things you might have asked, that will be the hardest. They are all clamoring to see you."

"I'll go to the desert. You can tell them I am recovering my strength."

"If you could appear for a moment, later in the day, and speak a word or two—"

"I'd spend all morning fretting over what to say and all evening wishing I'd spoken differently. Permit me one day, Peter."

"As you say."

"It's no pleasure winning an argument with you, my friend. I always lose in the turned-down corners of your mouth. Let me be self-indulgent tomorrow. My guilt will make me all the more diligent the day after."

"Of course."

"When we recast the world, everyone will be given your smile."

"Will you stay with us tonight?"

"No, I'll leave while it's still dark. I am a thief and must travel like one."

"What have you stolen?"

"A body. My body. I'm a grave robber. Though not so grave as you would like."

"I have no complaint."

"For that I am as grateful today as I have been for three fine years. On this one day I can be sentimental, can I not? That should be a prerogative of the dead."

"Do you have pain?"

"I ache. I felt faint, but the air has cured me. I must go."

Christ dragged himself slowly from the cave so that the others would not see him leave. When he was out of sight of the camp, he was tempted to rest, but he kept lifting one heavy leg and then the other. He stumbled two miles across the sand before he fainted.

When he recovered, dawn had begun to lighten the darkness. He lay on one heavy yellow blanket, and another blanket

covered him. Someone—a man—sat beside him, shivering in
the cold air. This man leaned forward and pushed his fat pink
face in front of Christ's. "Ah, you are finally awake, then? I
thought you were a late-bloomer, one of those men who sleep
past midday."

Christ turned away his head to yawn. "I'm sorry. I had a
strenuous day yesterday."

"You ask for sympathy." The man spoke reflectively. "I
have given you my blankets and my protection, and now you
seek my pity as well."

"I was trying—"

The man waved him down. "Trying is a dreadful habit. So
often it leads to success."

Christ said, "I believe there's an adage to that effect."

"You are a wit," the fat man said amiably. "How fortunate
for me to happen upon so rare a phenomenon. You are not,
however, a dandy."

Christ plucked at his frayed robe and regretted the gesture.
"I've never been much concerned with my clothes."

"A mistake, if you will permit me to say so. Clothing is our
chief disguise, and it should be a good one."

Christ propped himself on an elbow to look around. His
companion wore a pink tunic trimmed with silks of rose and
burgundy. Gold bracelets shone at his wrists and ankles, and
the curls on his head were tied with purple bows.

"I'm afraid my work," Christ said, "would not permit me
such—"

"Magnificence? I suppose I am fortunate—unique—in that
regard. My work demands it."

"And that work?"

"I am a leader of men," he answered with a smirk.

"It is not an enviable role," Christ said.

"It suits me. What do you do?"

" I am a carpenter."

"How useful! What do you make?"

"I recently laid a foundation which I trust will prove serviceable."

"Do you know what I need? I need a throne. I have one at home with armrests, but I've been putting on so much weight lately that I must practically grease myself to sit down."

"Perhaps we should make chairs as we make tables—with an expandable leaf at the center."

"You are a clever carpenter." His tone warned Christ to hold to his station.

"No, only a poor fool lost in the desert."

"Why, then you can come with me." A crescent smile lit his moon face. "We always have room for another."

Ah, Christ thought, I am very slow. My mind has never been quick, and I am tired this morning. But now I understand. I recognize you now. "Where do you come from?" Christ asked.

"Over there." He gestured vaguely. "It's really very charming."

"I'm sure it must be." To himself Christ added, What did you expect? Did you think he would have cloven feet, or that he would insult and revile you, or that he would spring from a crevice in the earth?

"Would you like to go now?"

Christ found himself more fearful than he had expected. "I'm a little tired. If we could rest for another minute?"

"Whatever you like. I could wipe your brow."

"No, please. Thank you." They sat together quietly, the fat man beaming at Christ, his smile saying, We shall play for a little while that you are sick or small and that I am caring for you.

"The sun seems unusually strong for so early an hour," the fat man said, mopping his own brow with a white lace handkerchief.

"The weather of late has been very strange," Christ agreed.

"Perhaps it's the tomb."

"Tomb?" Christ asked.

"Oh," the other said slyly, "I understand that a tomb was opened yesterday. Imagine all that dank air rushing out! It probably upset the atmospheric balance."

"I know little about such things."

"No," the fat man leered at him. "I forgot. You're a carpenter."

"Yes."

"Of course."

Christ broached a new topic. "Who leads the men when you are in the desert?"

"Ah, we have a detailed chain of command and a wealth of talent to draw upon."

"Still, you are probably anxious to get back. If so, I could rest here and join you later."

"That's not exactly the bargain, is it?"

Christ decided not to pretend that he didn't understand. "No."

"We'll wait here until you feel better. There's no hurry."

"No hurry." The heat was beginning to weigh on Christ. He felt as though a hand were pressing his head toward the earth. I'm not good at this, he thought. I can be strong and forthright and sometimes playful with the men. But I'm not trained for this tiresome cut and thrust. I had assumed he would be serious.

"I suppose," the fat man said, "you've worked out some kind of rationale for your existence." Christ had no words. The other bowed elaborately. "As a carpenter."

"Have you?"

"One does the best one can. One does not choose one's role."

They both fell silent. As minutes passed, Christ shook his head and wondered if he had been dozing. Across from him, his broad face glistening with sweat, the fat man was dusting flies from the rims of his ears. While they sat without speaking, a cloud of sand blew up on the edge of the desert.

"Someone seems to be coming from my camp," the fat man said.

"Your camp?"

"Oh, yes. Over there. We keep pretty much to ourselves. You understand."

Christ nodded.

A man came running toward them, apparently with some message. He staggered forward, almost falling from exhaustion. "Christ!" he cried. "Christ!"

Christ rose and started toward him before he saw that the messenger had been addressing the other man. The fat man saw Christ's response to the cry, and his belly shook with laughter. "Oh, no!" he exclaimed. "Not you, too? Not you! On the other side of the desert?"

"Yes," said Christ, confused.

"And all this time," the fat man said, wheezing and wiping tears of laughter from his eyes, "I thought you were the Devil."

Simon, who was softhearted, became indignant each time he recalled that Jesus had been made to bear his own cross to Calvary. To soothe him, Jesus said, "I was spared the fate of most men. I had been a carpenter, after all, and though they forced me to carry my cross, they did not call on me to build it."

During one triumphal entry into Jerusalem, a fair-skinned man thrust himself in front of the animal that bore Jesus. "Lord!" he called. "Do you remember me?"

"Certainly," Jesus responded warmly. Three years spent campaigning among the people had taught him to be politic.

"I was afraid you might not." The man, about fifty-five years old, bobbed his head gratefully. "You had only been on earth one day when I visited you."

That clue was enough for Jesus. Thirty years before, Melchior had already been old, and Balthasar was far darker than this pale man. "I am happy to see you again, Gaspar." Jesus dismounted to walk a few paces with the descendant of Ham.

"So often I had wondered what became of you," Gaspar said. "You have no idea how pleased I am that your promise at last is being fulfilled."

"Your good wishes are important to me," Jesus replied. "My mother still recalls your visit and the generosity of your gifts."

Gaspar hardly seemed to hear. He had sunk for a moment in a thought of his own. "You're Earth, aren't you?" he asked abruptly. "I'm sure that's right—Earth?"

"I was born of woman to traverse the earth and bring God's word to man," Jesus allowed, puzzled at the excitement in Gaspar's voice.

"No, I mean your birthday. You were born in the trigon of Earth?"

Jesus wondered if he had fallen in step with a lunatic. "I don't know what you mean," he said coldly.

"Astrology! The true guide to foretelling the future. Surely you are a believer?"

"I believe in the One God."

"But you must believe! It was the conjunction of Jupiter and Saturn in Pisces that produced the star that led us to Judea. You were heralded to the world through astrology."

"I was heralded through centuries of messianic prophecy."

Again Gaspar had withdrawn to his own thoughts. Lengthening his stride to keep up with Jesus, he started to rummage through his robe. "Let me give you proof," he said. "I will cast your horoscope from the stars."

"I foresee my future," Jesus said. "It is nothing I wish to anticipate."

Gaspar had already begun to consult the symbols painted on a parchment scroll. "You are right," he said awesomely. "The coming week holds many perils. It favors quiet evenings at the fireside with your family. New ventures should be postponed. Friends may prove difficult. Above all, keep your natural good humor."

Convinced that Gaspar's idolatry was harmless, Jesus began to tease him. "What can you tell me about next Friday?"

"Friday?" Gaspar studied the brightly colored charts and circles. "Friday is all right. In fact, Friday could turn out to be unusually propitious. If there's a day that should concern you, it's Sunday—one week from today. That's a day with a number of bad portents."

Jesus thought, His predictions are accurate enough. Friday I escape the world and Sunday I am compelled to return. These forecasts are designed for men, and men long ago set a low value on life.

Worried by Jesus' long silence, Gaspar asked, "What do you think of astrology now? It's not blasphemous, is it?"

"It's too accurate to be blasphemous."

"Do you mean that truth is always reverent?" he persisted. But Jesus had boarded his mount again, and Gaspar was caught in the midst of fifty children waving palm leaves.

As Jesus set out again on the journey, he opened his billfold, withdrew a manila envelope and read his sealed instructions:

Nothing above cabinet rank unless the population is less than three million.

Avoid Roman Catholic, Lutheran and Methodist denominations.

Be scrupulous in registering for the draft and paying overtime parking tickets.

College teaching only as a last resort.

Andrew approached Jesus abjectly for he clung to the idea that a savior had more important things to do than talk with him. And Jesus found the husky fisherman already so gentle that he hesitated to tamper with his spirit.

"Can I talk to you for a minute?" Andrew asked.

"Certainly, my friend. I wish we spoke together more often. You're too industrious."

"Just now I had a scissors, and I was cutting the hair from my nostrils." Andrew's heavy nose trembled from hearing itself discussed. "It's vanity, I know, Lord, but otherwise the hairs grow very long, and I would look ugly to your followers."

"I don't think you could look ugly to anyone. But if you choose to cut away some excess hair, there's no cause for apology."

"No, that's to explain what happened. I was standing before the mirror, my head thrown back, about to begin, when I looked deep into my nostrils, and I was afraid."

If Jesus had been about to smile, the sight of the man's white face and twisting hands would have stopped him. "Why?"

"I saw the dark openings, like tunnels into my head, and as I stared into their darkness, I was afraid I would see—"

"God?"

Andrew nodded and wrung one big hand with the other.

"You thought that the idea was blasphemous? That such a foolish fantasy was an offense against him?" Again Andrew nodded unhappily. "But you were looking into eternity. That's a logical place to expect to find God."

"Lord, I was looking into my own nose!" His voice rose in dismay. "My nose!"

"Yes, the thought is ludicrous. I agree with you. But logical, Andrew." Jesus cupped his palm and placed it lightly over Andrew's nose. "We don't pick our shrines. I wouldn't have chosen this spot, but I wouldn't have picked a lot of the damp grottoes either."

Contentedly Andrew asked, "Are you laughing at me, Lord?"

Wealth made no difference in either his task or his character. The first time he had awakened in a gilded crib, Jesus wondered if he would be changed. But the story was the same except for a slight variation that he first denied, then acknowledged and at last found he could accept without bitterness: All of them—his disciples, the multitudes, even his tormenters —liked him better rich.

Being handsome was less predictable. Sometimes he was plain, and those were the times he preferred. He spoke then and they listened harder because there was less to watch. The men's companionship was less flirtatious when he was plain. No matter how he looked, women gave him trouble. The leader is always desired; he knew and forgave that. Good looks, when they were given, were restrained. His nose would be more sharply etched, his mouth fuller, his eyes more deeply set. He never had to overcome a hairy, gleaming kind of beauty, and he was seldom disfigured. He taunted himself: Men want God's message delivered in a plain wrapper, and I am the one and perfect Messiah.

Downhearted, Matthew returned to Jesus. "A friend of mine says all of us are too normal to make an interesting book. He objects to your cures of Lazarus, the lepers and the lame. He says I have to include in my story one unstraightened hunchback, one full-grown idiot or one little girl with an arm amputated and the sleeve of her dress pinned to her shoulder. He says those people speak most truthfully for the human condition."

"In our way, we are crippled," Jesus consoled him. "Did you explain that?"

"He says that's different. He says there's nothing in our suffering to create sympathy in the reader."

"Not sympathy, perhaps. But we have been able to inspire self-pity, and that's a stronger emotion."

"Couldn't you arrange to encounter one blind and deaf mute and pass him by without restoring his senses?"

"Introduce me to your friend," said Jesus, and Matthew laughed in spite of himself.

"Have someone take care of this, will you?" Christ slipped off a torn blue jacket and let it drop to the floor.

Satan picked up the blazer and examined the two long rips in its left shoulder. He threw it to a tailor. "What happened?"

"Everything was going fine," Christ said. "No problems of any kind. We knew it would end early, but I figured I could make it to grad school anyway. We got the whole bunch admitted and settled in Wigg, which took some doing because, you know, some of those boys aren't mental wizards."

"I know."

"For once I thought it was going to be a good wait—everybody says it's usually so boring. You know, hacking around some machine shop or foundry for fifteen years."

"This is November. You couldn't have been there more than two months."

"It was Judas," Christ sighed. "He got eager and pushed me down two flights of stairs. That's how I tore my coat. Of course, the poor clod didn't realize he was wrecking the whole thing. The stairs were slippery, and I'm being listed as an accident. Some of the deans know better, but Judas can't expect them to speak up on my account. They've got the good name of the school to consider."

"Now what?"

"I spend the day here and go home. Someone else starts on Monday." Christ peered at Satan in the dim light. "You're young, too."

"I haven't been on the job long. It's something of a coincidence, your coming now. I used to do quite a bit of work at Phillips Brooks House."

"Is that right?" Christ looked dubious. "What kind of thing?"

"Games in the South End mostly—basketball, track."

"Gambling," Christ continued, "dice, heroin, petty theft—"

Satan said pleasantly, "You are even younger than you look. Do you want to come inside while you're waiting for your jacket?"

"Okay."

Christ followed him into a small room stacked with books and journals. Looking over the titles, Christ asked, "You were going to be a doctor?"

"Yes."

"That never appealed much to me. I'd figured I'd study philosophy and then go to law school."

"Useful."

"They're always trying, you know, to trick me." Christ's young voice broke. "They ask me all kinds of questions with hooks in them." He squinted to see Satan's necktie and asked, "Where did you get that?"

"It's from a club I belonged to," Satan said indifferently. "I keep it for sentimental reasons."

"Of course I disapprove of all clubs on principle. But I'd thought maybe, you know, until I really got started, I could join one for a year or two. Next year. I'd probably have picked that one." He waved toward the tie. "Unless you'd have had me blackballed."

"Why in the world would I do that?"

"Meanness." Christ was matter-of-fact. "To be disagreeable."

"I'm afraid you've got the situation backwards. If you'll recall, I was the one who was expelled. I seem to inspire bitterness, but I've never felt any."

"Why were you asked to leave?"

"I'll tell you. But I'd like you to promise not to repeat the story."

"That's dumb."

"I know," Satan said. "With the small difference in our ages, I feel ridiculous trying to protect you. All the same, it would be awkward for both of us if you repeated the story after you left here."

"All right."

"First—and I don't say this to belittle you or to hurt your feelings—I was put on earth for the same reasons you were."

Christ ran a hand through his long blond hair. "You mean you had the same job?"

"Almost identical. We hadn't picked out all of the disciples yet—you were ahead of me there. But the pattern was no different."

"I don't understand," Christ interrupted. "I went over the whole album—at least the last ten years—and I didn't see your picture."

Satan laughed without malice. "No, I'm sure you didn't.

We're all the same: We only keep records of our successes. I'm not going to enter your name in our files down here either."

Something in his words caused Christ to shudder, although Satan's tone could not have been friendlier. "Why are you here then?" he asked reluctantly.

"It's a mistake in strategy to give us both the time and capacity for reflection." Satan had turned toward a lamp where a book lay open, and Christ saw the clean strong lines of his profile. "That may have been why your assignment was curtailed. It's one thing to put a naïve boy in a woodshop for fifteen years. To get the same degree of obedience is much harder if you've locked him in a library."

"Obedience?"

"What would you call it when the pattern of your life is so rigid that you don't dare break it? You wouldn't suggest that that's freedom. After four years of study, I found myself valuing freedom above all else." He smiled to himself. "And here I am."

"Why do you sound proud? The reason to be free is to choose goodness. Since I've been granted perfect goodness, what do I need with freedom?"

"There are people who value knowledge above sanctity. There are people who will accept no obstacle to wisdom, no matter whom they must defy. These people are all here, and I was honored to join them."

"Adam and Eve," Christ scoffed. "They're really old-fashioned. Nobody cares about them any more."

"You wouldn't say that if you knew them. We have great respect for their courage and initiative. I'd like to have you meet them, but just now he's working in a laboratory in Shanghai and she's in the London Foreign Office. The next time you're here—"

"This is my first time and my last, remember?"

"Of course—" Satan shook his head.

"What?"

"No, never mind. If a man can't control his thoughts, at least he can hold his tongue." When he saw that Christ was prepared to let the matter drop, Satan added quickly, "I was only going to say that you would not necessarily have to leave."

"Stay here?" Christ's voice rose an octave.

"You know what you're going back to. Those gilt halls and overpainted ceilings. What would your friends at school have said about them?"

Christ surveyed the small study. "I don't see that things are so good here."

"No mansions. But no laws and no lawbreakers. We do as we like, and you will say that means licentiousness but you'll be wrong. After the first week, men forget all the temptations that restrictions breed. They start to use their freedom as they never could on earth. You'd be a lawyer, matching yourself each day against the finest advocates of all time. Of course, you can run from here instead and go back to that drab dictatorship where talent is smothered and extraordinary gifts are punished as heresy.

"Ordinarily I wouldn't offer you the choice. I have not been impressed by the caliber of my immediate successors. But you have the capacity to appreciate what I'm saying. Our talk today has convinced me that you'd be an asset to us."

Christ wondered afterward what he had been about to say. Before he could speak, the tailor reappeared from an alcove, carrying his blazer on a hanger. Christ took the jacket to the light. "Incredible!" he exclaimed. "You'd never know it had been torn at all. It looks like new."

Satan said smoothly, "When I spoke of excellence, I didn't mean merely intellectual development. Our craftsmen work incessantly to improve their skills. I'll show you—"

Christ had slipped into the coat and moved toward the door. "I think I'd better be going," he said. "Thanks for everything."

"You wouldn't care to spend the night and think over what I've said?" The humility in Satan's voice softened Christ's reply. "No, I don't think I'd better. They'll be waiting."

"We could have used another good lawyer." Satan released the catch on the door.

"You don't have to—" Christ stumbled on the threshold. "I mean, you don't need anybody else. Not the way you can talk."

"Too bad I wasn't a bit more eloquent. I was thinking of your own good, you know."

"Oh, yes, I know. And I appreciate it. But—" Christ spread his arms helplessly.

"Habit is hard to break," Satan said kindly, and Christ nodded. As the boy began to climb the steep flight of stairs, Satan returned to his room. He took pains to shut the door gently behind him.

Marching to the closet, he ripped off his Oxford-cloth shirt and striped tie. Then he pulled hard at the bell for his valet. The man appeared at once. "Yes, sir?"

"Return these to Thayer," Satan snarled.

"Thayer Senior, Junior or the Third, sir?"

"The Third, of course! Naturally the Third! Thayer Junior wears wing collars."

The servant withdrew, and Satan pulled on a tight red sweater that set off the thick muscles in his shoulders. He combed his hair, longer now and darker, to a point at the back, bared his perfect teeth at himself in the glass and grinned at his own vanity.

Flushed and dancing with excitement, the slim youth burst into the railroad car. He sat across from Jesus at the window and reveled in his own reflection. They were alone in the compartment. After three or four minutes had passed, he looked up and said as casually as he could manage, "I just killed a man."

"Did you?" Jesus laid aside his book.

"An old man. I pushed him off the train."

"Your father?" Jesus asked, before he could think better of it.

"No, a stranger. I bore him no malice. I killed him to affirm my free will. It was an act perfect in its amorality."

Within a generation Jesus would hear the same argument from poor and ignorant boys in many cities. But at this point he associated such behavior with the wealthy and the middle-aged, and this young man in his threadbare coat surprised him. "I have restored men to life," Jesus said. "That, too, was a gratuitous act. Why must you prove your theory with death?"

"I cannot give life, but I can take it away." The boy looked uneasy. He seemed to have expected Jesus to call the conductor.

"The fall from the train killed the man. You only pushed him. You could do as much to help a man regain his health. I think the real trouble is a deficiency of imagination. Our new philosophers don't see that an unmotivated good act can also be shocking."

The boy got up to leave the compartment. As he threw back the door to the corridor, he spoke from between clenched teeth. "You take the fun out of everything, don't you?"

God seldom rewarded Jesus. Only on occasion, when an assignment had been especially well handled or when Jesus' spirit had fallen low, would God grant him a boon. One such moment came at the banks of the Jordan after Jesus had confronted and subdued some of the Baptist's fanatical associates.

What do you wish? God asked at midnight when everyone was asleep on mats under the black sky.

I want to penetrate the darkness, Jesus answered. I want to see what lies behind the night.

You will be disappointed.

I am not so young that I expect majesties or glory. I only want to part the curtain and let it fall closed again. I expect nothing.

Your wish is granted, God said. But you cannot thrust your hand through darkness as though it were the velvet drapery across a stage. You must peel the night, and the task is long.

How do I begin?

Reach up your fingers and touch the air. Pull gently.

Jesus followed the instruction. A layer of film, translucent and weightless, settled over the camp.

Again.

Jesus pulled away another layer and watched it fall across the earth. He took another, a fourth, fifth and sixth, before he stopped to inspect his work.

The night is no lighter, he said. I can only pull away bands of radiance, and I am not touching the darkness.

Blackness is one bright film laid on many others.

How many others? Millions?

I have not counted.

So you are also the darkness if we are patient enough to persist.

And you are disappointed after all.

I hoped to learn a single gesture.

A more dramatic way.

Instead, you ask for a patience that must end in failure.

What do you have to do that is more important?

Nothing.

Reach again and stop your counting. The failure ends when you give up the count.

At the instant the heavens parted, the Baptist turned up his face and absorbed the words with his whole being. "This is my beloved son—" the Baptist's eyes shone with pride— "in whom I am well pleased." John dropped his head with humility and looked for long moments into the depths of the brown river.

This will not do, Jesus thought. Apologetically he said, "I believe he meant me."

More to pass the nighttime hours than in the hope of making converts, Christ appeared in dreams to men on their deathbeds. For some he had a word of reassurance. Others were permitted to ask a question. "You may proceed," he said to an expiring figure on a hospital bed. "Is there anything that troubles you?"

In the voice of a man nearly dead, the question came: "Was the Last Supper the paschal meal eaten on the fourteenth of the Jewish month Nisan or another meal taken on the thirteenth?"

Christ had learned to meet provocation with civility. "Did you understand me? You have only one question."

"That is my question."

Bending nearer, Christ asked, "You are a professor of theology?"

"Yes." The voice was weak but proud.

"The synoptic tradition?"

"Yes, yes. I have debunked the Fourth Gospel on that point, but now I worry that I will be proved wrong."

To soothe him as he tried to recall which date was correct, Christ said, "I don't believe that you can be refuted." Before he could speak again, the old man made a sign that he was content and died promptly to forestall further disclosures.

Jesus had been perfect. He waited confidently for thirty years and then, when no call came, lived out the remainder of his life secure in the knowledge that any fault had not been his.

"What has given you such trouble?" Jesus asked a querulous Paul.

"For one thing, your apparent soft spot for prostitutes," the preacher answered. "Women in my congregation find that tolerance hard to understand."

"Your mankind baffles me, too. They could have taken any one of a dozen virtues and made it supreme: honesty, kindness, generosity. Instead, they have chosen chastity, for which they have no talent, and they have defined sin as little more than sex. Since I don't share their obsession, I can't accept their priorities."

"I point out to them that you have condemned promiscuity."

"To make them listen I affirmed a few of their prejudices. When you have come to burn down the house, you don't object to feeding a fire on the hearth."

"Some women have hinted at an episode in your past."

Jesus smiled into his cupped palm. "I am the Son of Man to the waist and the Son of God to the ground. I might have devised a better message and converted more people if the order had been reversed."

"Don't say that to my women. You'll shock them."

"I tell them the most shocking thing of all: that faith can

bring eternal life. Because that truth doesn't involve sex, they are never very interested."

"You hold a low estimate of my women." Paul spoke with some annoyance.

"Only in my mind."

Jesus sipped his beer slowly and tried to overhear the conversation of the two men on his right. Ten days earlier, the younger one had been acquitted of murdering a woman who worked for unpopular causes. Jesus said to himself, All right. I've seen him now.

"Hey, mister," the other man called over. "How about having a drink on us?"

Jesus shook his head and made the gesture of being bloated with beer. The youth sitting on the stool next to Jesus swung around, and his companion said, "My name's Danny. And this here's my cousin, Billy Joe. I reckon you know who he is?"

Jesus shook his head.

"Aw, come on. Where you been?"

"I got to town today."

"You don't read the papers?"

"Not much," Jesus said.

"Well, maybe you're right there. They all but one of them told a bunch of lies about Billy Joe. They were trying to say that he killed a woman, a fine lady visiting our little city here." The man's laughter roused his cousin, who joined in. "We're still kind of celebrating," the man said. " 'Course the jury didn't believe any of those lies about old Billy. They knew he was away in—where were you when some varmint struck down that fine lady, Bill?"

The youth pushed his empty glass forward for another beer. "I don't rightly seem to remember right at the moment, Mr. Prosecutor."

"Anyway now we all got to be patriotic citizens of this great country and go out hunting for the real killer. It must have been somebody with a pretty good aim, I figure, because he picked her off driving about thirty miles an hour and with the sunlight against him. Somebody, I figure, who just couldn't understand why he didn't have the right to defend his home and family. Do you know anybody like that, Billy?"

"They're getting worse." Ignoring the other man's question, he pounded his fist on the wooden counter. "When I think that right this minute they're down at their dirty headquarters, and they're—"

"Never mind, Billy." He threw an arm around his cousin's shoulder. "We're going to take care of it."

"I'm going, too."

"Not this time. Wait a spell and trust your cousin Danny. We're not going to let you down. You're a hero. I hear a lot of folks saying that. They say for the first time in years you made them proud again to be a man."

Jesus pushed aside his beer and walked out of the tavern and back to the bus station. All right, he said to himself. All right. All right. But don't let them remember to repent. All right. But don't let them repent.

When she took his hand, he pulled away in embarrassment. "Think of Martha," he said, flustered, "in the kitchen."

I'm getting too self-centered, Jesus upbraided himself. It occurred to him that for weeks he had worried only over his own comforts. His kindness had been perfunctory, and for a long time he had not been touched by another person's sorrow or joy.

Because he was nineteen, he could go on sparing himself. But he saw these early years as a time for practice and experiment, and he resolved to begin that day.

The proof of his indictment was that, once he had determined to do good, he was not sure how to begin. Misery surrounds me on all sides, he told himself, but I haven't been seeing it. I must open my eyes again to the world.

With nothing more definite in mind, he walked briskly to the square, sat on a bench and began to watch the people. Next to him was an old woman with her face turned up to the sun. Jesus leaned over. "Excuse me." She opened her eyes and tightened her grip on her purse. "What is it?"

"I wondered if you'd like a drink?" She stared at him with such disbelief that he added, "A soft drink or something? I'm going over to the stand, and I could bring one back for you."

"Beat it," the old woman said.

As he loped away, Jesus smiled to himself. Exactly the right answer to an insipid suggestion. I'm not some kind of messenger boy. Look for true need.

He rested for a minute on a low brick wall, enjoying a light breeze that brushed the heat from his cheeks.

"What time is it?"

Jesus looked at the man at his elbow: about thirty, stocky in a black crew-necked sweater and white trousers. "I don't have a watch," Jesus said pleasantly. "I think it's a little past noon."

"Nice day." The man had moved closer, and he was looking intently at Jesus.

"Very fine," Jesus agreed. "Are you new to the area?"

"I been in town a few days, but I don't know anybody here. Nobody at all. It's kind of lonesome."

"You'll find that it's a friendly place. You won't have any trouble meeting people."

"I hope not. I had a lot of friends back home."

Jesus had the feeling they were touching. But when he

looked down at the railing, their legs and hands were a foot apart.

"For the time being I'm over at that hotel." The man pointed to a modest building at one edge of the park.

"Nice place," Jesus said.

"Have you been in there?"

"I've never been inside. It looks comfortable."

"Why don't you come up for a little while? I've got a bottle, and we could have a drink."

Must I help him? Is this a need he's showing me? Or is it something else, an indulgence? I don't want to turn away from anyone I could help. But sometimes to help best is to turn away. "I guess I'd better not. I'm supposed to be home in about five minutes."

The man did not seem disappointed. "Okay," he said, pushing off from the wall. "Another time."

"Good-bye." The man did not answer.

Jesus stayed another hour and listened to the story of a woman whose lover had left her the night before. "What'll I do?" she kept sobbing.

"He'll come back."

At last, to comfort Jesus, she pretended to believe him.

On his way home, Jesus saw the man in the black sweater again. He had a bald man gripped by the elbow and was steering him toward a police car hidden in the bushes at the end of the park. Well done, Jesus said under his breath. When it comes to diligent rehearsal, I can still learn a lot from Judas.

The night's last call had come from a woman who threatened to kill herself. By the time the station left the air, she had stopped sobbing and agreed to call Jesus again the following night. He signed off and went to the cubbyhole where he stayed most mornings until dawn answering his mail.

"Nothing like ending with a bang." Nate Weinstein, an engineer, came in to sit on his desk. "Do you hire people to call like that?"

"I suppose I do. I'm on the air every night for five hours advertising for misery. They supply the problems and I give them an audience. It's a straightforward transaction."

"Why?"

"Why what?" Jesus had begun to type with two fingers.

"Why do you put up with it? You could have any job at the station, right?"

"I've been trained. I could do most of them, I suppose. Probably not too well."

"So why?" He spoke with the urgency of a thirty-year-old man missing everything that had seemed ordained ten years before.

"This is important."

" 'Let's Talk'?"

"I reach more people with one program than I did in three years of lectures."

Nate took another tack. "But doesn't it all depress you?" He grabbed a letter and tore it getting the envelope off. "Here's a girl who's going to have her second illegitimate child and her father has threatened to kill her. She wants to call you Thursday night. Can you put that aside when you go home? Doesn't it start eating into you?"

Jesus had given up typing. "What's the choice? These problems won't go away because I drop the program. I might not hear about that girl except later in a police story, but whether she talks to me or not, she's going to be pregnant. This way I might help a little. Not much."

"And that's why you're the most cheerful guy at the station?"

"I wasn't aware that I was."

"Oh yeah, everybody's noticed it."

"I don't want to be a distraction."

"Look at you now—from ear to ear. You're hopeless."

"Hopeless," Jesus repeated.

"Anyway—" Nate Weinstein was not as jaded as he tried to sound. He'd go back to his control room and snort to himself for the rest of the night. "I still say it's no work for a grown man."

"Grown men have been busy growing," Jesus said. "I don't expect them to do my job."

Nate Weinstein said witheringly, "Save it for the sponsor."

In one of the hot places people go to take the sun, Beirut or Torremolinos, they had gathered around a hotel table and were watching an old woman who had entered the lobby with a fairly young man.

"That's sad," James said after the man had made it clear he was not her son. The others put down their wineglasses and nodded, but John smiled and shook his head.

"That's what we say now, isn't it? That it's sad or pitiable. That he should be ashamed or she should act her age. Why? She has him for a week or a month, whatever she can afford. And he may not love her. But he loves money and what money buys. Would it be less sad if she came in alone? Ate alone, drank alone, slept alone? Or if he stood outside the hotel envying the thick bath towels and the tall cold drinks? Does their double unhappiness add up to more than their separate unhappinesses?"

James said, "You know you think it's degrading for both of them."

"It would be nicer for us to watch them if she were young and he were rich. But look at him: He's smiling at her. He may like her. She may give him something, besides the money, that he could never admit he needed."

"You're presuming, of course, that they're both unmarried."

"She's widowed or divorced, and he's making some young girl on the other side of town very unhappy. But not married, no."

"You're still opposed to adultery?"

"I've never liked the word."

"Then you're not going to rewrite everything?"

"Not this afternoon."

"What John was saying," Nathanael put in, "is only what Jesus has said, 'Let those who are without sin—' "

John interrupted. "I suppose he said something like that. He's said so much. But I never liked that phrase either. I can't see why a man should search himself for the license to condemn others. Jesus should have told that man to search others for a reason to forgive himself."

James said irritably, "Not only are you rewriting, you're ruining the style."

Jesus, who had been quiet, said, "We'll ask Luke to patch it up. Where is he?"

"In Hollywood."

"Working?"

"He's writing the script for a Western. He says they're the new morality plays."

"I'm not much of a horseman," Jesus said. Remembering, they laughed with him.

"That's all right," Nathanael said. "You'll have a double for the dangerous parts." At the expression on Jesus' face, they laughed even harder. Wine and the sun were warm on their lips.

Jesus had trouble persuading the people of Epsilon Eridani that the Earth was not their Biblical Hell. He assured them that explorers from their star had exaggerated the Earth's faults and that these distortions had been magnified by news-papermen and real estate developers. He made his point, and drew a nice laugh, when he reminded them how amused they'd be if the people of Earth thought Epsilon Eridani was Heaven.

She called after midnight to ask that Jesus come to see her right away. He was staying with friends in the hills, about twenty minutes by car from her estate. "I'm sorry to call so late," she said brokenly. "You know if I didn't have to I wouldn't."

"I know."

"At your age—" she began, in a tremulous voice half the world recognized.

"Don't worry about me. Put on your record album."

"I broke it."

"You shouldn't have done that. I liked to hear it."

"I can't sing that way any more."

"And I can't tell stories the way I used to. But I don't forget the ones I've told."

"Oh, no!" He had frightened her. "Don't ever do that!"

"I won't. I'll even think up some new ones for you."

She laughed softly. "Isn't it funny? You're the only man I'd like to have."

He taunted her as he always did when she strayed to that subject. "It's safe enough to say, Mary Magdalene, to an old party with white hair and false teeth."

"That hog tonight wanted—"

"Forget about him. Brew some cocoa for us."

"I don't have marshmallows."

"I'll bring them. This time get the water hot enough."

"How domestic I am for you."

"We'll draw pictures." He was groping in the dark for his shoes. "Do you remember how you liked to do that?"

"Oh, yes! Hurry!"

"I'm on my way."

He put down the phone and turned on the bedstand lamp. I have tried so often to save her soul, he grumbled to himself. These days I'm content to save her life.

Matthew had prepared a list of rebuttals to questions the interviewers might ask. A few minutes before air time, Jesus looked through them. "I see you refer here to the serenity and calm so often seen on the faces of nuns and priests."

"Everybody's noticed it and commented on it," Matthew explained. "Men of every religion or no religion at all will remember seeing a nun on a streetcar, and they'll find themselves agreeing with what you say."

"I tried that argument once. It was at a time long before television, and the Frenchman with whom I was debating then asked if I had ever seen a dead body. There, he said, was true serenity, true peace. I was only extolling the living dead. He found beauty in the ravaged faces of men who had given themselves to life, not those who had escaped from it. A religion that condemns suicide, he said, has no right to establish monasteries."

"What did you say?"

"I answered, but my reply was too involved for the program I'll be on today. In those days men lived half as long, and they could be prodigal with their time."

"If they do ask about monasteries, what will you say?"

"I'll turn the conversation to leprosariums and orphanages and hospitals and schools."

"Ah," Matthew sighed, "you're much too worldly for us."

Although his title was minor, the position Jesus held within the palace allowed him to watch visitors arrive at court, and he was not surprised one afternoon to see Mary Magdalene ushered into an antechamber. He bowed before her.

"You look good, Jesus." She would not release his hand when he lowered her fingers, and he felt the full weight of her rings on his palm. "When is the uprising? Should I alert the king?"

"Years distant," he said. "I would think that you disturb him enough with your beauty."

"Courtliness comes hard to you. I wonder if we'll ever find an age that is comfortable for both of us."

"Eternity."

Playfully she dropped his hand as though she had been burned. "You speak too heavily," she reproved him. "You will never make a decent courtier."

He bowed again before her. She accepted his dismissal and began to move with her attendant to the door of the throne room. Almost on the threshold, she returned quickly to him and whispered, "Don't be harsh with me. I need your good wishes more now than when I was dirty and poor. Don't let your friends judge me cruelly."

"They cursed you then from fear. Now they convince themselves that what you do, you do for gold, and they curse you from envy. Envy is innocent. I let them abuse your name."

"Must you?"

"Would you rather be poor again and frightening to them?"

Mary Magdalene made a fist to show Jesus the rubies and diamonds that covered the skin of her fingers.

Jesus disliked crucifixes, but he saw little hope of eliminating them. He wondered, though, why they had chosen to commemorate the one helpless moment in his life, the single time that the world had acted upon him. What would he

have preferred? He considered the choices: A sentimental
statuette with a stray lamb slung over his shoulder. A bronze
of him lifting a cripple to his feet. A statue of the resurrection, with only marble stigmata to show what he had suffered.
Instead of these, mankind had chosen the cross. As a symbol
of guilt? Or pride?

"Do you know what I hate?"

"No, John," Jesus asked with an air of elaborate indulgence,
"what do you hate?"

"I hate the way they all look over at you before they
laugh."

"I hadn't noticed."

"Even before they dare to laugh, they want your approval."

"You may be right."

"You don't even have a very good sense of humor."

"Is that true? I thought I did. I thought I had to have."

"Be serious. What have you ever said that was funny?"

"That's not the test. I stop them from laughing at things
that aren't funny."

"You're proud of it! I can tell! You are actually proud of
the way you stifle everyone. Why are you laughing?"

"You're funny, John. You're funny enough for both of us."

John, who had begun to laugh, stopped suddenly. "I think
I just looked at you before I started laughing."

At thirty-four, Mary Magdalene was getting thick around
the waist, and wrinkles were starting to show up where her
chin joined her neck. She held a responsible job at a large
insurance company as head of the fire and flood section. Few

women achieved anything higher than the post of chief assistant, but Mary Magdalene was a good worker, conscientious to
a fault, and she had been with the company sixteen years.

Jesus liked her because she insisted on perfection and because she smiled when she asked the others to correct their
mistakes. She brought Jesus hard-boiled eggs in her lunch bag.

As he took the eggs, he would say, "I thought the bars had
stopped serving these. Look at them all. You must've hit every
night spot in town."

She'd blush. She lived quietly with elderly parents. "That's
right. The Tip-Top. The Surcease. The Better Late. All of
them."

"One of these eggs has Easter dye on it."

"That's from the Better Late."

"Of course."

The other women liked her for a simpler reason. She had
never married, and they could pity her behind her back while
they pretended to believe her hints of past romances.

Sometimes the secretaries suggested that Jesus invite her to
dinner. "Mary Magdalene likes you, Jesus," they'd say. "She's
still a good-looking girl. Why don't you?"

I'll accept her lies, as the others do, Jesus decided. I'll let
her be wicked by word of mouth. Passing her desk I won't
speak words she fears—"virgin," "pure." But I cannot provide
her sins, no matter how the other girls plead her cause. They
expect too much from me these days. They must still do their
own sinning. I don't ask that they enjoy it.

Jesus opened his notebook on the study hall desk. Using
the ruler from his geometry class, he drew a ledger's line down
the center of one page. At the top of the left-hand column he
wrote "Assets" and over the other, "Liabilities." Under "Liabilities," he printed in block letters, "Impatient."

Shielding the page from the girl across the aisle, he added:

Demanding
Self-righteous
Proud
Moody
Suspicious
Filled with doubt
Tend toward arrogance

With some dismay he counted the entries and began to contemplate the "Assets" column. With another look to be sure the girl couldn't see the page, he wrote, "Son of God."

In better spirits, he closed the notebook and started on the next day's translation of Cicero.

As I have done faithfully since the requirement was first imposed, I now submit this report on the episode recently concluded. My enthusiasm for the task is lessened somewhat by the heavy editing my last report underwent. I am aware that the need for popular acceptance makes some change essential, but I continue to believe that an accurate recounting of our efforts serves our cause better than the gilding and gelding to which my previous account was subjected. Its subsequent success with the public in no way changes my opinion.

I regret having to begin in so disputatious a way. We have been through a difficult time, as you know, and I find that I have not fully recovered.

I am inclined to attribute part of the blame to our previous performance, hailed and applauded though it has been. The injection of political considerations led to a number of unforeseen complications and proved to be a heavy strain on Jesus. He had expected to be tried and executed again by the religious community; over the months he had readied himself

for the traditional stoning. When the Romans became involved and the manner of execution was changed, the effect
on him was unmistakable. I had covered all this in the previous report so that, while my protest was vetted from the final
text, you are aware of my views. I repeat myself now only
because lingering effects from the preceding episode obviously
compounded our problems.

As has been my practice, I am omitting in the interest of
brevity all prefatory material. Having complained of your editing, it is fitting and fair that I should remark favorably on the
introduction prepared in your offices. I appreciated the bow
to our distinguished tradition in the phrase, "In the beginning
was the Word." The transition to matters at hand was grace-
fully effected with, "And the Word became flesh and dwelt
among us."

The felicity was marred, for me, only by the unnecessarily
extended passage on John Abijah, also known as the Baptist.
Yet I am forced to admit that my reaction may be colored
by a personal aversion to that crude individual. Certainly the
literary competence of the introduction, far beyond my most
ambitious efforts, exempts it from further criticism.

Our adventure started in an ordinary, even sluggish, fashion.
Your instructions to Jesus seemed to impress him deeply although he felt that your reprimand for his complaint on the
cross was harsher than the remark warranted. In his defense,
let it be said that Jesus has at no time denied having spoken
the unfortunate words. Although—and this is the very last
objection I'll raise—I note that his words were excised from
my text. I hope that, in the interest of historical accuracy,
they will be restored to later editions.

He also pondered long your injunction that he treat his
mother with greater respect. While I have made every effort
to ingratiate myself with that woman, I can understand that
she might prove something of a trial to her children. At any
rate, he seemed to agree that he had been brusque with her in

the past, and he told me that he intended, from that point on, to act the model son.

As I say, the early stages passed uneventfully. Physically, Jesus had often been more impressive, but he was in no way deformed. My own appearance was something of a disappointment to me. You will recall that on previous occasions I have been well built, rather small, with curly hair and the large dark eyes that I had come to regard as fitting accessories to my role. They had all but defined my temperament as amiable, impetuous, lighthearted and loving.

On this occasion, however, I found myself as thin as a herder's crook and at least as gnarled. I was eight years older than Jesus and three inches taller. Any thought of resting my head on his chest was ludicrous. So my physique may have contributed, in a very limited way, to the series of events that followed. I have long believed in the importance of appearances and have found that those who scorn good looks are either the stupidly beautiful or the enviously ugly.

In the course of several months, we acquired Peter, Andrew, Philip and the rest. Peter at least upheld our traditions by being the eldest of the disciples. This steadying influence was undercut by his character, of which I will be compelled to say a good deal more.

Jesus at this stage was undergoing one of those despondent periods that we have learned to expect and endure. Mindful of your directive, he tried, despite his moods, to treat everyone courteously, and he seldom railed at us. A memorable exception came when he overheard Nathanael ask the ironic "Can anything good come out of Nazareth?"

We had never considered his question more than a gibe intended to show the common, even despised, nature of Jesus' childhood surroundings. Yet, on this occasion, Jesus marched to the young man's side and said, "It ill behooves anyone from a town as wretched as Bethsaida to talk about Nazareth."

Startled by the challenge, Nathanael began citing statistics to prove the importance of his home. Jesus responded lamely with those few boasts that a Nazarene can make. He told of a fine cow that had won renown three years before and of a certain silversmith who enjoys good, if limited, reputation. At last he broke off and strode away.

Nathanael was ashamed at prolonging the argument and called after him, "You are the king of Israel!" But Jesus did not look back, and he was slow afterward in accepting the youth wholeheartedly.

Perhaps we should have taken more notice. However, life with Jesus has never been easy, and we disciples have learned to accept those rigors of temperament that accompany rewards of the spirit.

One fine spring day we walked to Cana for the wedding of a good friend of Jesus' family. The bridegroom was a large and nervous fellow, already losing much of his black hair. His bride was comely, if more ample through the hips than either fashion or biology required. Mary, the mother of Jesus, had arrived the night before and was all but running the ceremony.

"There you are, John," she called when she spotted me. "I thought you would never get here. Come and help me with these flowers." She was braiding them into a garland for the bride, and I held the yellow and white blossoms until she was ready for them.

"The garden looks beautiful, doesn't it?" she asked. "We were up most of the night decorating."

"Very lovely."

"Is my boy all right?" she continued in the same preoccupied way. Through unpleasant experience, I had learned to be guarded in what I confided to her about Jesus.

"He seems to be. We're all tired from the journey."

She plucked a bit of greenery from my hand and wove it through the flowers. "That's good. There's been some talk that he was acting strange."

"Strange?"

"Strange, John," she said testily. "Peculiar. I would have thought you'd know what the word means."

"Certainly I have heard it before." I ignored her implication. "But never applied to your son."

"It's probably nothing but gossip then." She concentrated on pinching withered leaves from a blossom. "What does my son say? A prophet is without honor—" She waited for me to finish the phrase, but I only nodded.

Other guests had begun to arrive. When Mary dispensed with my services, I sought out Peter. From the time of our first meeting, I had felt some responsibility for him. "Hello, John!" he shouted. "Can you see the spot on my coat?"

I inspected his festive white tunic. Near his knee there was a large dark blot. "It's hardly noticeable," I said, in the hope he would not spend the afternoon repeating the question to each of the other guests.

"I knelt to pray where a camel found relief before me," he beamed. His red round face, so bland, so inoffensive, could rile me until I ground my teeth.

"Why don't you look more carefully, Peter?"

"Perhaps I am losing my sight," he answered cheerfully. "I may be the next recipient of a sign from our master."

"There have been no signs as yet, and you know we are forbidden to anticipate them. I am often amazed at your lack of discretion."

"Yes," he agreed. "Perhaps, instead of my sight, I am losing my mind. Of course that would be more of a challenge for Jesus. Who could prove afterward that he had cured my head?"

"Who indeed?" I said crossly.

Philip joined us as the party began moving into the garden for the brief ritual. "I didn't expect to find you here," he said with his unfailing smirk. "Not with the fishing fleet in."

"You are a tiresome young man," I said.

"To you, I suppose I am," he answered archly. "I am sorry I'm not equipped to be more diverting."

"I have no regrets." Turning to Peter, who was blushing and smiling with particular vapidity, I said, "The ceremony is about to start. We must join them."

"I was married for twelve years," Peter recalled. "I was faithful part of the time and she was faithful part of the time. Unfortunately, they were never the same times."

"She died of fever."

"Yes. Have I told you?"

"Once or twice."

The service was soon over, for which I was grateful. Unworthy as it may be, my resentment at weddings has always run high. The fact that family and friends could gather to endorse and applaud a bedding made me resent all the more the furtive nature of my own pleasures. When the words had been pronounced and the couple's lust made legal, the reception began in the courtyard. Warmed by the last rays of the afternoon sun, I went to the garden's far wall and sat for a time by myself while the bridegroom's wine splashed from wooden barrels. When the last cask had been emptied, I drifted toward the crowd that was trying to wring a final drop from an upturned rim.

Jesus was watching with a look that, only afterward, struck me as unusual. At the time I thought he was bored. Later, recalling the pallor of his face and the way he rubbed his wrists, I wondered if he might have been frightened.

"I'm afraid we are out of wine," the bridegroom said, wiping a heavy sheen of sweat from his brow. I couldn't help looking toward Jesus, who had moved near three barrels of water that stood beside the wall. Gingerly he dipped a finger into each of them. Nathanael, who also had been watching, joined him by the barrels and peered inside. "Why, here are three more large casks of wine!" Nathanael exclaimed.

"Impossible!" the bridegroom said. "That is only water. I drew some of it myself this morning."

"You are mistaken," Nathanael replied confidently. "It is wine." He seized the dipper and took a large gulp. Unaccountably he grimaced, coughed and spit the murky liquid to the ground.

Peter and I had run to his side. As Peter slapped his back to end his choking, I picked up the dipper Nathanael had thrown down, and I took a cautious sip. Only an effort of will kept the new wine in my mouth. It was as sour as vinegar.

Peter, who had watched my performance attentively, took the handle from me and drank a long draught. When he finished, his eyes looked red and moist, but he smacked his lips and drank again. "Delicious!" he proclaimed. "It is that excellent new wine with none of the cloying sweetness so distressing to a cultivated palate.

"Wait, friends," he called to a group passing him. "Wait until you have tasted the treat our host has been saving for us."

The young men and women paused before him. Talking all the while, Peter ladled out a glass of the rank stuff for one girl. "I should not give you so much, for this will be a hard habit to break. None of that sickening aftertaste of sugars. Only the piquant flavor of the grape, picked at the precise moment that the juices are fresh and not yet corrupted by the poisons of earth and vine."

By this time the unlucky girl had swallowed the wine. Her mouth puckered into a dozen folds and the veins in her neck stood out blue and red. Finally she spoke. "Marvelous!"

With the help of two youths, one of them very well built, Peter moved the wine to the center of the court. There he continued to talk rapidly and reassuringly to the guests before they had their chance to drink. As a result, only one old woman fell to the ground, gasping and trying to eat dirt.

Otherwise, the wine was sampled by everyone and extravagantly praised.

The bridegroom followed in Peter's wake, explaining that he had run out of wine and that Jesus had transformed these barrels from water. "How?" someone asked.

"By calling on God for the miracle," I said hurriedly. It would have done no one any good to have explained that he had dipped his hands into each barrel, particularly since his fingernails that day were not notably clean.

In the excitement, Jesus himself had been forgotten. I found him sitting on the secluded wall I had earlier discovered. "Your wine is a great success," I said.

"I do the best I can," he answered sullenly. "I'm no vintner."

"You will not get an argument from me. My tongue is still blanched from the mortification."

"They have to be tolerant, too," he said with a vague gesture. "I'm expected to forgive everything. But they don't try to understand me. It's not all easy."

"No one said it was."

"You're like the rest of them, aren't you?" He looked at me coldly. "Don't trouble yourself. I'll go through with it. I'll do it all."

I was impatient with him and, strangely, I was thirsty for another sample from the last barrel. Any wine improves in age and bouquet with a second glass. "If I can help you, Lord, it would be my greatest privilege." I left him then, but I was glad afterward that I had spoken.

In the week that followed, Peter became insufferable. "Did you hear what I told them?" he would ask. "I am such a goose usually. I can never find the right words, and yet I saved the entire day, didn't I?"

"There's another wedding next week. Jesus could try again there."

He did not seem to hear me. "Do you think God inspired

me, John? What other answer could there be? Here I am, a foolish old man who always says the wrong thing, and yet I was magnificent. And do you know? I didn't have any idea what I was going to say. The words just spilled from my mouth. Do you think it was a miracle, John?"

"If so, a very small one."

"It may be the pinnacle of my life," he said with great solemnity. "I may never reach such heights again. If that is true—" his soaring spirits fell—"it came too soon, didn't it? Now the rest of my life will seem shallow, barren, not worth the trouble of continuing. Oh, God!" he cried. "Why was I not shielded from youthful success?"

"You are," I leaned heavily on each word, "fifty-three years old."

"I am but a babe in Jesus." When he rolled his eyes piously, I was led perilously close to blasphemy or violence.

For all his moodiness and prolonged periods of silence, Jesus had not failed to draw crowds. The young, particularly, were attracted by his intensity and his evident misgivings. I seemed to be alone in my concern that we were not gaining that diverse support we need for a well-founded success. To my colleagues, our crowds seemed as large as they had ever been, and the response was sometimes even more boisterous than in the past.

Wary of innovation, Jesus waited for the precise moment to travel to Jerusalem for the Passover. Even with our attempt at strict timing, however, there was an irksome mix-up. With spirit and indignation, Jesus had driven the money-changers from the temple before we learned that they were actually clergymen staging a harmless fund-raising game. One woman who had five coppers in a row across her card and was prepared to claim a prize became implacably estranged from our cause when Jesus kicked over her table. She later sought damages for her losses and for an unsightly red welt across her shoulders that she claimed had come from Jesus' whip. Peter found a neighbor to swear that the mark had been left by a beating administered by her husband, and she stopped bothering us. Still, the episode could hardly be considered a triumph. While we were occupied with raising money for fines and settlements, Jesus withdrew even further from us.

Weeks passed with almost no public appearances, despite ample opportunities to address sympathetic groups. When I could remain silent no longer, I went to Jesus early one evening and sat uninvited at his side. Had I been able to fall upon his neck, whimpering and cajoling, perhaps he could have been roused from his despair. I could only draw my robes around my bony knees and speak forthrightly. "Are you praying, Lord?"

"No."

"Would you like me to pray for you?"

"If you like." He was neither courteous nor rude.

"You are worrying all of us."

"I don't mean to."

"You're not still brooding about the fish and barley loaves?" He did not reply. Faced with the feeding of a multitude the previous month, Jesus had not produced the required rations. How serious an attempt he had made, none of us could say. As the day dragged on, Judas Iscariot took funds from our collection box and bought food for the audience. Though they may have been grateful, the people did not confuse generosity with prophecy.

Since my interview with Jesus was going poorly, I was relieved to be joined by his mother. Mindful of your instructions, he made an attempt at gallantry with her, but the effort was beyond him. "Hello, Mother," he said. "I hope the night air is not too cold for you."

"I've got on my new coat." She waved an arm so that nearby firelights caught the coat's gloss. "Very expensive," she said to me. "Of course the other women are jealous, and they're saying the most disgusting things."

"It's handsome, Mother. I'm glad we could get it for you."

"It's little enough," she said defensively. "I've never asked for anything for myself. Did you ever hear me ask for anything?"

When Jesus did not answer, her question hung over both of us, and so I said, "A silver buckle a few weeks ago—"

"It's not for myself," she went on, ignoring me. "I need these things because of my position. It wouldn't be right, with my son the most important man in Galilee, for his mother to go around looking like the village slattern. If you want respect, you must command it. I've told my husband that a hundred times."

She had seated herself on the cowhide Jesus spread for her. For a minute we all stared over at the fire's flickering lights. Then she said to Jesus, "I've come to find out what's the matter."

I made no effort to leave them, and neither seemed to want me to go.

"I'm tired tonight, Mother." It was more a plea than a rebuff.

"From working so hard?" she asked sharply. "From running all over the countryside, bringing the word of God to people who need it so badly? Is that why you're tired?"

"You know I haven't spoken lately."

"I know you haven't." Her voice softened. "What I've come to find out is why."

"I'm resting. I'll start again. Everyone shouldn't be so worried."

"We should have faith?" I asked.

"I'm talking to my son," Mary said, not disagreeably. She was on the verge of reaching for his hand when Jesus moved it to his knee. "I know what I have to do and I'll do it. That's enough."

"It isn't enough for me," his mother said. "I don't understand the way you're talking. You sound like you've been

given some dirty chore to do. How can you talk like that?
Don't you know that you're lucky? You're the luckiest man
on earth, and here you are sulking as though your life was
ruined."

"I may not think I'm so lucky."

"You sound like a twelve-year-old, my son." Her manner
had changed again, and the kindness was congealing. "You
are no child being fitted for his first tallith. You have seen
enough of life to know your duty. Don't think I don't understand your complaints. I do. But I don't understand that they
should come to you now, fifteen years late. To a child, duty
can seem very hard. I was fourteen when I first learned of
your coming."

Jesus did not speak.

"After I knew, I cried every day. I wasn't a girl who wanted
to be singled out. I had thought that I'd grow up and get
married. I even had my husband picked out, the son of
some friends of my mother's. I didn't want much, and I didn't
need camel's-hair coats or silver buckles. I wanted a home and
a husband and some children—healthy, not sick.

"I couldn't tell anyone why I cried. I'd go out on errands
and hide behind a wall and cry for an hour. But after a few
months there wasn't a wall big enough to hide my belly, and
that's when all the putting up began.

"For the next thirty years I didn't do anything myself. I just
put up with things. I put up with marrying the first man who
would have me. On the day of our marriage, I almost ran
away. But by then the other boy didn't want me. I had no
money and no place to go. So I got married. I started to learn
something. I learned, for my husband's sake, not to cry. And,
for my sake, he learned not to ask me every hour of every day
who the father was.

"I put up with my husband, and he put up with me. I put
up with neighbors whispering when I passed, and I put up
with their children laughing in my face. I put up with Joseph's

parents. They wouldn't speak to me until you were almost three years old." She stopped and laughed to herself. "Maybe I didn't know when I was well off. But in those days it was hard. I'd pass them every day, and Jacob would look away and his wife would look right through me and never say a word.

"Before you were born I used to dream of how I'd treat them all, to make up for what they were doing to me—which ones would burn in hell, which ones would see their own sons drowned or with their throats cut open. But I didn't tell them about you because I was too afraid. I was sure you'd be born dead or mute or, worst of all, that you'd be ordinary. Once after we came here, I tried to speak to a woman I thought was friendly and tell her about Bethlehem and the star. When I got done, she looked at me and said, 'But there wasn't so much light when he was conceived, was there?'

"And she told the other women, and at the market they started to call me Mary Moonshine.

"But by then all those dreams about paying them back had stopped. The night you were born, all of that drained out of me. Or most of it, to be truthful, because I do enjoy boasting a little about you and showing off my new coat. But I can't hate them any more.

"When the first signs showed in you, my joy was so big I felt pains in my heart. Even then I didn't tell anyone. I was so afraid something might happen to spoil it. Now you're set on the path, and the people who laughed at me come to my house and they let me know without saying anything that they're sorry for their laughing.

"My days of putting up with life are over. For the first time in thirty years I look forward to getting up in the morning and going out of my house and meeting other women at the well. You've lifted my shame from my shoulders."

We sat silently again, Jesus between his mother and me. She said softly, "Don't make me start putting up with things

again, son. Don't let them say that Mary's bastard was a false
prophet."

She got up with some difficulty, for she was a bulky woman,
and she brushed at the hem of her coat. "Is it so terrible that
I show off my new coat?" she asked. "That's not such a big
sin, is it?"

"It might be worse." Jesus smiled at her. "But there'll be
no coats in heaven."

"None at all?" she cried. "Not even a little scrap of goat-
skin in the evening for the shoulders of the mother of the
Son of God?"

"The animals will need their skins, Mother. Unless you
can persuade a goat to curl around your neck."

Mary shuddered. "No, I'll get along the best I can. No
place is perfect, I suppose."

"You'll be happy," he said.

"Do you promise?"

"I promise."

"And will you be happy here? For my sake?"

"I will try."

"Do you promise?"

"I promise that I will try."

She looked sternly at me. "Sometimes I wonder if someone
around here isn't putting all these depressing ideas in your
head. You're contented, aren't you, John? You're not stirring
up trouble?"

"Stirring up trouble is part of our job, you'll remember." I
was polite, perhaps I even bowed slightly.

"Yes, I know that," she said impatiently. "I'm trying to be
sure that the rest of you are taking care of my son."

"We do what we can."

"He's very important, after all. He's—"

"Mother," Jesus said, "I am tired. Perhaps tomorrow we
can talk again."

Mary kissed him briskly on the cheek, hesitated, then kissed my cheek, too. "Good-bye," she said. "Remember what I told you, John."

When she had gone and we were alone, I said, "Your mother is right. You are very important to all of us."

"We'll go out tomorrow," he said wearily. "Tell the others. I'll speak in the afternoon and in the evening."

I was pleased, of course, but would not be put off. "My situation makes it easier for me to travel with you," I said. "I do not have to leave a wife and children to join you. But my nature makes me desperate for you to succeed. You are my one hope."

"You will not be disappointed."

"You don't approve of my life, I know."

"I approve of you, John," he said. "I don't confuse you with your life."

"I will not disappoint you either." I spoke with more fervor than I had ever experienced. "You have saved me, and I will help you to save yourself."

He rose slowly, his young body as stiff as mine from the cold and damp. "We think we do everything for others," he said. "But it's only that the others know what is best for us."

"Thank you, Lord," I said as we parted.

For the next four months our progress was steady and strong. Jesus continued to be in no mood to experiment, but he delivered the traditional words with great persuasiveness. Afterward, with us, he went to considerable lengths to be obliging, even cheerful. The change had inspired all of us, except Peter. He watched everything warily, his great obtuse face wrinkled from the strain of thinking.

"Isn't it fine now?" I asked him one day.

"Now," he nodded glumly. "Now it's fine. How will it be later?"

"If you wanted guarantees," I replied, "you should have stayed in your old business."

"You haven't seen what I've seen. You're a young man,

John." For that observation, I could forgive him his denseness.

It was at a meeting soon afterward that I took extended notes because I heard Jesus departing for the first time from his prepared text. Later my notes were confiscated, and what I record here is a mere outline. The departure began when someone challenged one of the parables—the prodigal son or the payment in the fields. Jesus had often been chastised for offering a reformed sinner greater honor than the man who never strayed.

This time I recall that he began by saying, "I have heard it said that I teach slavery and submission. That is not true. I offer a doctrine of mastery—mastery over the only slave worth subduing, mastery of a man over his own spirit.

"From birth some men are generous and kind, gentle and good. Or they have been given natures that permit all virtues to be implanted early and harvested throughout a lifetime. In saying this, I do not disparage the meek. Their rewards will match their merit.

"But there are other men who are not mild, men who hate fiercely and forever, men who strike when struck, men who see no meanness in revenge. Those are the men whose return to God sets off such great rejoicing. Among the others, who are good without effort, there should not, cannot, be envy. They have been spared temptation and, for that, they sacrifice the triumph.

"So do not say among yourselves that God cares only for the pure or welcomes only the innocent. God loves all men. If he can forgive me, there is none among you who cannot be saved."

Well received though they were, these remarks were taken as nothing more than new proof of Jesus' humility. From subsequent events, we know that he was offering us a warning. But who broods about the dark edge of a shining sky or the first chill of a summer afternoon?

All that I have written so far is preamble, of course, to the events six months later. Over the years, Jesus had come to have great affection for Lazarus and his two sisters. To me, this Lazarus, at twenty-six, was hardly more than a child, with a child's extravagance of moods. He was clever and well read, but he would often cry: "Why is my life so tasteless on my tongue? Why am I too comic for tragedy and too sad to play the clown?" He reminded me somewhat of Peter, although, of course, the older man had never realized the extent of his own foolishness.

At any rate, Lazarus was one of those youths convinced that the seeds of their greatness were being spilled on the barren soil of the age. Jesus had often warned him against worldly pride. But even Jesus had succumbed to a vehemence and verve that were equally amusing whether the boy was magnifying his talents or deprecating his fate. His sister, Mary, was a slight, pretty girl who worshiped Lazarus. In his presence she rarely said a word but sat quietly, even when everyone else in the company was shouting with laughter over his complaints. The eldest in the family, Martha, was a goodhearted woman who found her brother lazy and criminally wasteful of his gifts. She wanted him to be a rabbi. But he stayed at home, lamenting that the era of great rabbis had ended. Sometimes, only to torment her, he would intone in a nasal but pleasing voice, and she would rush to the neighbors, crying, "Did you hear that? Ah, what talent that boy is throwing away!"

Because Lazarus took such immense pleasure in his unhappiness, we seldom made an effort to cheer him. In fact, Philip could generally cite new reasons for despair and goad him to greater breast-beating. We were not at all prepared, then, for the news that the boy had consumed a poisonous herb and was nearer death than life.

As our instructions required, Jesus expressed confidence in a quick and full recovery. "He will not die," he told the messenger who brought the news from the sisters. "This is another test for me, and I will meet it."

But the two ritual days he had to pass before returning to Bethany were an evident trial to him. He was pale and distracted. Finally, on my own initiative, I canceled an evening appearance by explaining to the crowd that Jesus was deep in spiritual communion. He chided me for my interference but left no doubt that he was relieved.

The next morning we proceeded to the town at a clip that brought us to the outskirts by noon. Martha was waiting on the road to greet us. Mary, she said, was too faint to leave the house. A large group of their relatives had gathered on the front stoop, and in the distance we could hear their wailing.

"He would never have done this if you had been with him, Lord," Martha said. "You gave him courage."

Jesus assured her that Lazarus would live. At this point she may have known already that her brother was dead but would not accept the fact. Seeing her hesitation, Jesus taxed her with disbelief. She responded with the usual protestations of faith, but the furrows in her brow and despair in her voice belied her words.

While we waited on the road, Martha ran to fetch Mary. In twos and threes the relatives began to approach us, and it was from one of the boy's aunts that we learned he was dead.

Jesus did not weep. But he withdrew from us, and he did not hear Peter assuring everyone that Lazarus and Mary would soon be reunited. "They will be together again as they have always been," he cried in a tone not unlike that of the gatekeeper at a carnival. "Side by side!"

One of Lazarus' cousins, a short-haired sniffling boy distraught with grief, ran to Jesus to demand, "How can you heal the old and useless and let our kinsman die?" Jesus did not answer. His concentration at that moment was greater than I had ever seen. I would not have been astonished if the skies had cracked or the earth changed color. Instead, in the gathering darkness, we waited. When Mary did not appear, we drew nearer the house.

"Open the door," Jesus said. No one obeyed him. The old people at the gate said they had heard terrible sounds inside and they were afraid to go closer.

Followed by a few of us, Jesus stooped to enter through the small door. In one corner, crying out in tongues of grief, Martha had collapsed over two bodies. Mary had fallen on a knife, and she lay at her brother's side, blood pouring from her breast.

The air of purpose that Jesus had assumed fell away at the threshold. His eyes were dry and he uttered no sound; but something passed out of him.

"Bury them," he said, and he lifted Martha away from the bodies. They went together to the kitchen, where Jesus set her to making bread. She asked him many questions, but he shook his head and helped her knead the dough.

Peter had looked briefly upon the scene and then had run from the room. We could hear him calling along the road, "A miracle! A miracle! Lazarus and Mary reunited! Together as they have always been! A miracle!"

I said to Jesus, "I'll make him stop," and he nodded.

By the time I had run Peter down and clapped my hand over his bawling mouth, the bread had been brought from the oven.

That night Jesus disappeared. Without him, we occupied ourselves as best we could and waited. He had been gone before for many nights, and we assumed he was alone on one of the mounts or terraces of the desert. Those men who could fish returned to their boats. I fell into something of my old ways despite the handicap of my uncongenial appearance. Coming as they did after my conversion by Jesus, these excursions caused me great remorse. Yet, without his physical presence to sustain me, I have never been equal to temptation.

One fresh spring morning Jesus returned to us. He had scraped away his beard and cut his hair far shorter than was our custom. I had expected him to be lean from his long fast, but he was well filled out, and as glossy and bright as the early sun. When he saw us, he laughed and waved a greeting toward the tents down the road where an undaunted multitude had awaited his return.

"Ah, Matthew!" he called. "And James. How are you? You seem to be flourishing without me. I should have stayed away longer."

We clustered about him, vying for his attention and remarking on his own good appearance. He suggested that we have a banquet to celebrate his return, and my brother, James, who had little talent for anything else, was put in charge of the arrangements. The preparations, as well as Jesus' high humor, unsettled me. But I could think of no cogent reason to protest.

Philip, who was not always insensitive, caught my arm as the homecoming festivities continued and said, "We're moving fast, aren't we?"

"He's the one who knows when the time has come." I spoke with little conviction. "It's not up to us to judge."

"Cautiously put, John," he said mockingly. "But you must admit the whole atmosphere smacks more of fatted calf than of wine and wafers."

"I often wonder," I said, "how you came to be included in our number."

"My father's family lived next door to Joseph's father," he admitted readily. "I don't think I would have made it otherwise."

"Try to be kind to him tonight. If there is another failure, we may lose him completely."

"For you, John," he teased.

Outside our circle, I would not speak of this, but the washing of feet has always been one of the most distasteful duties of our calling. The occasion usually embarrasses everyone but Jesus, and I have seen Simon, for one, weep with chagrin that his Lord should be kneeling at his feet. In my own case, I grant the significance of the occasion while deploring its necessity. And yet the solemn moment has been further spoiled by the distaste I feel for anyone touching my body. Apart from the caresses of love-making, I loathe feeling another person's hands on me and this distaste, I regret to say, extends to the savior.

The ritual is generally performed, after Peter's demurrers, in complete and shamefaced silence. For that reason the uproar that accompanied this latest re-enactment was all the more surprising. First Jesus insisted that we drink a number of toasts before he began. They were frivolous but not offensive, and our room echoed with happy, perhaps somewhat self-conscious, laughter.

With the beginning of the washing, that laughter rose to an unseemly pitch, for it developed that the bottoms of Peter's feet were extremely sensitive. As Jesus knelt and took his foot, the old clown first shrieked and then began a series of helpless, gagging yelps.

Jesus took all of this with immense good spirit, and I thought that, when the old man's screams were subsiding, I detected him tickling Peter's arch. I won't recount the rest of the proceedings, which verged on travesty of our sacred obligations. We had become so afraid, I think, of our Lord's prolonged melancholy that we entered into his games more enthusiastically than was proper.

At dinner I leaned near him. "Lord, who is it?" I prompted, since he had not yet mentioned the next step.

"Who is what, my friend?" He thrust a dish of meat at me. "Eat some more, John, you're getting far too thin. And more wine! We must rejoice tonight."

"I asked who it was who will betray you."

"Betrayal," he repeated. "Do you remember what I once

said about mastery? There is only one betrayal that matters."
He dipped a morsel carefully. Then as we watched, he swallowed it himself. "You will seek me," Jesus said after a moment. "But I must tell you, where I am going you cannot come."

Peter asked, "Lord, where are you going? Why can't I follow? I will lay down my life for you."

Jesus smiled broadly but said no more. We waited impatiently for his lengthy speech of exhortation, that outpouring of love and trepidation that had always ended our supper. Instead, Jesus poured out wine by the cask, joked with each of us and seemed oblivious of or indifferent to the final act of our drama.

After midnight he at last arose and led us to Gethsemane. The night wind was cold enough to cause us to huddle within the grotto and wait there for the end.

Within the hour, Judas appeared with a band of shamefaced soldiers. Some of them I recognized from our meetings. Without a word, Judas pushed through us, grasped someone firmly in his embrace and kissed his cheek. As I moved for a closer look, I saw that he held Peter in his arms.

The soldiers looked puzzled, but they surrounded Peter with their swords drawn. I tried to find Jesus in the gloom of the cave, but he seemed to have slipped away.

"Whom do you seek?" Peter asked hoarsely.

"Jesus of Nazareth." The captain of the guard had lifted a lantern to scrutinize Peter's face.

Peter did not speak for a long time. He, too, was looking in the dark corners of the cave for Jesus. When he saw no trace, he murmured, "I am he."

The soldiers who had known Jesus fell away in astonishment; but the light was bad and Peter's voice, though low, was firm. More confidently Peter asked again, "Whom do you seek?" Again they answered, "Jesus of Nazareth."

Peter spoke now with a peremptory note, "I have told you that I am he. So if you seek me, let these men go."

Still moving with some hesitation, the guards began to jostle Peter off to the priests. The old man had recovered enough of his composure to be unnerving to the rest of us. Whenever he caught my eye, he would wink broadly. And on the way out of the cave, he stopped for a minute beside an Arab slave to fondle his ear.

"My friend," Peter said to him gaily, "you don't know how lucky you are."

I followed behind, down the vale and up a slight incline to the walls of the city. Since we had managed to avoid any political involvement, Peter was taken directly to Caiaphas, and he was to be tried and sentenced in the religious court. I wondered later what Pilate, a man of cultivation despite his weakness of character, would have made of Peter.

The captive was still bouncing along with his guards, chattering and laughing, when I drew alongside. "Be of good cheer, John!" he shouted.

I scowled, worried that his imposture would be discovered and discredit our cause. My sternness did not seem to affect him at all. When a cock crowed, Peter threw back his head and echoed triumphantly, "Cock-a-doodle-doo!"

Of course the guards thought he was mad. Since they found little pleasure in tormenting a man who did not frighten them, Peter was spared the beatings Jesus had usually received.

With the dawn, all their misgivings about Peter's identity returned. Caiaphas, who held the post of high priest only through the influence of his father, was short of sight and wit. Yet even he suspected that a mistake had been made.

"If you are Christ, tell us," he commanded in an uncertain voice still seeking its pitch.

Peter said, "If I tell you, you will not believe."

"Are you the Son of God, then?"

I must admit that Peter appeared to have some scruple against this blasphemy, but he proceeded faithfully with his duty. "You say that I am," he said smugly.

The high priest's father, Annas, hardly knew of Jesus, and he asked, "Is this the man who is such a menace to our faith?" Embarrassed, Caiaphas replied, "I will prove it, Father."

He sent out for any member of a temple who had heard Jesus speak but had not been converted. As we waited, guards strung a carpet between two posts so that only Peter's head could be seen. On either side of him, the priests put soldiers and servants until there were seven heads in a row, Peter's the second from the right. Every one of the others looked more like Jesus than the old man did. They were younger, more serious, infinitely better-looking. I avoided Peter's eyes for fear he would launch again into his frantic winking and grimacing.

When the preparations were complete, the guards ushered in an old widow, a woman I had seen occasionally at our meetings. Jesus had been gulled by the old crone, even to misinterpreting the contemptuously small contributions she donated to our cause. But I recognized the sheer malignancy in her withered face. I do not think it is entirely my proclivities that have led me to the conclusion that the softest spirit in the world is that of an adolescent boy, while the toughest is lodged in the shriveled breast of an old woman.

She stamped along the marble corridor, peering up at each face with unbounded hatred. Her one regret seemed to be that she could not indict all seven of them. When I dared, I looked up tentatively at the scene.

The soldiers and servants were flushed, their eyes downcast. As she paused in front of each man, his body went rigid behind the screen and his mouth tightened with obvious guilt. Only Peter looked innocent. He beamed at the woman and rolled his eyes to heaven as though contemplating the purity of his soul. He was so friendly, so open, so genuine, so sweet, submissive and guiltless that she cried, "That's the man!" and the guards cut down the carpet and seized Peter with new assurance.

The sentence, to be carried out immediately, was pronounced. I had barely a moment to speak to Peter before he was led to the courtyard where executions were held. "Take this scroll, John," he said. "It may be useful."

I hid the worn leather scroll under my tunic. "I'm sorry," I said.

"For what?"

"That I did not recognize you."

He laughed and waved his fat pink hand. "We should know by this time that we can never be sure. But we forget, don't we?"

I did not witness his death. A servant told me later that he had behaved well, even to calling out, "Forgive them, Father, for they don't know what they're doing."

One of the first stones stunned him, and his agony was brief.

That evening we had considerable trouble with Judas Iscariot, who was stubbornly refusing to hang himself. The others finally called upon me to go to his tent on the outskirts of the city and try to reason with him.

He seemed to know the purpose of my visit. As I approached his fire, he called, "You're wasting your time!"

"Where is Jesus?"

"He should be well on the way to Rome by now," he said.

Judas is hardly the most attractive of men, and his air of belligerence did not improve his sallow looks. "He's left a lot of money for me," he volunteered. "I'm a wealthy man."

I crouched by the fire, saying nothing.

"Peter didn't have to die," Judas said. "He could have

proved that he was not the Christ. I didn't expect him to be killed. It was his own fault. He didn't have to die."

"You know better than that."

"I don't care. I have enough to live in splendor for the rest of my life. I might even go to Rome. Jesus suggested it. I might go there and live with him."

"No."

"You can't scare me, John. I have money now. Nobody can scare me any more."

"Brother," I said, though the word passed reluctantly through my lips, "aren't you forgetting your reputation? What about that?"

"Reputation?"

"You are the greatest villain in history. You know you enjoy that."

He thought for a moment or two. "I will like being a wealthy man in Rome better."

"Nonsense! Nothing can compare with being Judas Iscariot. You know your name will outlast all of ours."

"Perhaps," he said, almost coyly.

"But if you live, what then? You may repent. Think of that. You are sure now that you won't. But your liver goes and your bowels loosen, and a man who betrays a friend can betray the younger self whose youth he envies.

"Or say you do not repent. How can you know that a good deed will not cheat you of your fame? You could save a child from drowning—a simple, unthinking act—and historians forever after would amend their judgments: 'Although as a young man he betrayed Christ, Judas partially redeemed himself five years later when, without regard to his own safety, he plunged into an icy creek—' You can see what that would do to you.

"Or say that you succeed in living a cold, mean, selfish life. It is a difficult road to choose, but people have managed to do it. You may find at eighty that the popular view of you will have been reversed. Quite rightly, men regard long life as penance, as punishment enough for any sin. Petitions will be signed to rewrite the records and absolve you. Kings will mark your final birthdays and saints will weep at your bier."

"You don't know all of that."

"I can't prove it," I answered. "But you cannot take the chance that I am right."

Not looking backward I left him, and I was reassured that he neither laughed nor called after me. Later that night we heard that he had done the right thing.

By the time I returned to Jerusalem, Peter had been laid in the sepulcher, his old carcass rubbed with perfumes and oils. Late Saturday it was apparent, to me at least, that there was to be no resurrection. I was forced to turn to Philip because his faith, while tenuous, was of a nature to accept this final setback.

Saturday midnight we removed Peter's corpse from the cave and buried him outside the south wall. When this disagreeable chore was done, I posted Peter's scroll on the entrance to the tomb and went back to my quarters for a long sleep.

The sun was high in the sky before my brother came bounding to my bed. His phlegmatic spirit was frenzied with excitement. "He has risen!" he shouted. "The Lord has risen indeed!"

"Did someone see him?" I have learned not to underestimate mass hysteria.

"No, no one has seen him. He has left a message for us all."

"How do you know it's from Peter?"

"Thomas brought a friend of his who knows handwriting. He swears it is genuine."

I yawned and slipped into my sandals. "We must go to see," I said wearily. "You are convinced that the message is from the Lord?"

"Oh, yes!" James said fervently. "This is the best day of my life!" He is not a bad boy.

At the tomb were eighty or more people, shoving and shouting. I forced my way to the front and took my time reading the message again.

Peter must have written the note some months before, possibly even on the night of the wedding party. It explained that he had risen from the dead, had toured briefly through Hell and had intended to return that morning to Earth. Urgent business in his father's kingdom, however, compelled his immediate return and, to his great sorrow, he was forced to postpone indefinitely his reunion with us.

There followed an exhortation to preserve the faith and to trust in God. The entire effect was almost exactly right, and I only wished Peter had consulted me before he wrote it. I could have helped him with the spelling.

The yellow convertible had not been designed to be inconspicuous, and during the first hour they spent in town Jesus spotted it on a parish parking lot. By the end of their second day Peter had completed his investigation of the minister who drove it.

"He's very popular," Peter reported to Jesus. "They say that if he had not become a minister, he could have been a highly successful businessman."

Jesus nodded.

Peter knew they could expect trouble in each town from the authorities, and he saw no advantage to antagonizing the local clergy. "He's apparently been very effective at helping men to stop drinking," he continued. "He's increased his congregation tenfold, and his special collections for overseas missions are the largest received from this region."

"The car was presented to him by a grateful flock at a testimonial dinner on his last birthday." Jesus liked to exhibit his powers of deduction.

"That's right. He was consulted only about the color."

"He turned down red as unseemly."

Peter glanced through his notes. "I don't have information on that."

The long shiny car was parked across the street from where they stood, and Jesus went over to examine it. "Newly waxed," he observed. "No dents. Telephone. Air conditioner."

"In presenting their gift, the president of the men's club said it was only fitting that the man who represented God should travel as comfortably as the man who represented the gas company."

"Was he right, Peter?"

The old man shrugged. "We've been through this, Lord. It might be better if every minister were happy to live in a hovel, eat dried crusts and walk miles on his daily rounds. You haven't always approved of those men either. This minister is admired for his energy and compassion. Those qualities might count for as much as his bad taste in automobiles."

"It won't do, Peter." Jesus had pulled out a large pocket knife, and he kneeled by the side of the car. With one solid blow, he slashed the right rear tire and pushed the point of his knife through the gash to puncture the tube. He strolled around the car, pausing to rip open each of the other tires. "He can walk for a day," Jesus said when he had finished. "There are rules for God's house and for God's messengers."

Peter shook his head.

"You used to consider these excesses of mine cruel. Then you decided they were melodramatic. I'd ask you to remember, Peter, that tolerance is the passion of the indifferent."

His straining after epigrams grated on Peter, but he said only, "You can't slash the tires of every minister's expensive car."

"I can remind myself that the fury of a spurned God burns,

however dimly, in my breast. I can remind myself that in an age of thin, swinish love I must hate the lame who lack the faith to rise."

"I suppose that's to be the theme of your sermon tonight."

"As a matter of fact, I shall speak on God's gentle and infinite mercy. One of your troubles, Peter, is that you try to make things simple."

They walked toward the center of town, Peter wondering how, without adding to the scandal, he could reimburse the minister for his tires.

Joseph had asked Jesus to hand him a tool. When the boy was slow to obey, the old man grabbed it for himself. "I'm sorry," Jesus said. "I am finding that fourteen is a hard age for greatness."

"I don't remember," Joseph answered.

Jesus built a cabin by a pond where he lived in harmony with squirrels and woodchucks and the thrushes in a nearby wood. The experiment ended the day he tried with a brown bear the same tactics that had won over the woodchucks. His coaxing and affection brought him a slashing blow across one cheek and then, when he turned his head to forgive, the other. The wounds proved fatal.

Some time later Christ told this story to Luke, who labored four or five days before deciding it could not be developed into an instructive parable.

Nathanael grabbed his arm and pointed to another pushcart heaped with wood carvings. "Have you noticed?" he asked.

"They always make you look like Don Quixote." Even when he had repeated his question, Jesus did not deign to answer.

Jesus had been served many last suppers, and he made a point of asking his disciples, his guards or his enemies, "Will you eat with the same pleasure tomorrow when I am not here to share your food?"

Shamefaced or belligerent, all agreed that they would.

"Good," Jesus said. He seemed to mean it, and yet the survivors felt that their answer had diminished them in some way. The next morning they would try to leave favorite portions untouched on their plates or to experience some discomfort as they swallowed.

"He was certainly wicked," James said about a man they had known. "God will be harsh with him."

"How much would you punish him—" Jesus looked up from a manuscript he was copying—"if the judgment were left to you?"

The rich anticipation left James's voice. "I know his history, and I think I understand some of the reasons for his actions, so I would have to be lenient."

"Does that mean you consider God less informed than you are or less compassionate?"

"Only less human."

Jesus made a misstroke near the end of a page. "That was a good answer."

When Jesus bit his fingernails to the quick, the skin around each nail bled before it hardened into a callus and formed a hood over the fingertip.

His mother succeeded in confronting him after the night shift ended. He had spent all day out of the house, hoping that when he returned she would be asleep. In the morning he could leave a note and avoid her for another day. But she had waited for him, whispering her welcome so that she would not disturb the rest of the family.

"You should be in bed." He kept his voice low.

"I wanted to talk with you." Hard work had squeezed away the delicate qualities he remembered from his childhood. She was old and mannish. "Your sister has been crying all day because of what you said to her."

"She's not my sister."

"She is my daughter."

"That gives her no claim on me. I told her the truth about her life, and she could not deny that I was right."

"Why must you be so harsh?"

"Is that what you think?"

For warmth she wore a wool robe, and she sat tracing its faded pattern over the tops of her knees as she spoke. "Yes, that's what I think." She nodded her head.

Jesus spoke even more softly. "I give every energy to being kind and selfless, and I care enough about that girl and every other woman and man to spend my life among them. I have not said a fraction of what I believe for fear of frightening them or destroying their will to live. I walk about in a sickening guise of gentleness and piety, and you say I am harsh."

"We are weak creatures," she said. "We may not be worth saving."

"You say that I am harsh?" he repeated, his voice held low. "At the worst times I have never thought that."

"People would rather have love than truth."

"Then let them love one another if they can. God knows they can't be truthful."

"I told your sister you would apologize."

"Is that how I'm to show my love? To lie again to her?"

"It's the way she'll understand."

He did not understand why this woman had been chosen to bear him, but whenever he thought of her ordeal, his anger lifted. "I've caused much unhappiness in this house," he said.

"You have brought us joy."

"There must have been times when you wished that you had not been burdened with me?"

She did not look up from the interlocking circles in the fabric of her robe. She traced an arc and asked, "Do you want me to speak from truth or love?"

He felt nothing at her response, only a twinge in his chest that told him he would not apologize to his mother's daughter.

Soon after assembling his disciples, Jesus began to call attention to his own bulky sandals. He encouraged a certain amount of banter about their cheap construction and cumbersome design. Then, reluctantly, seemingly against his will, he shared the laughter that his sandals inspired, until every man felt free to make a joke at their expense. He was profiting from one of his earliest lessons: Always give them something unimportant to laugh at. Before they find something for themselves.

"Do you enjoy being famous?" asked one who loved him.

"Sometimes."

"It wouldn't be enough by itself?"

"No," Jesus said.

"I used to think it would be. It wouldn't matter why they knew me. To have everyone know my name would make up for everything else."

"It makes what you lack more important."

"I know that now. You know what taught me? Watching you."

"How?"

"I'd watch you with the crowds. They all loved you, but afterward you were alone. I knew if I were you, I couldn't bear it. I couldn't stand getting all that love and not having anyone to give it to."

"What about God?" Jesus asked.

"I don't mean that. I mean the physical love those people gave you. The way they wanted to touch you, the hem of your coat, the back of your fingers. That's not God's love, and it has to arouse the man who receives it. It must excite him. Any man would feel it."

"Any man."

"I knew then that I didn't care for fame, at least not if I didn't have the other."

"The outlet."

"It seemed to me that I could serve that need for you."

"That was before you knew me."

"I thought I knew you. I thought you were waiting for me. Do you know what I'm talking about? It's not stupid?"

"I know what you're talking about."

"I've embarrassed you."

"No," Jesus said.

"Do you love me?"

"I love everyone."

"Me?"

"Everyone."

"That's enough for me now."

John was difficult. His loyalty and talent were unquestioned, but other members of the staff resented his claim to a special

place near the ambassador. At last, after a very trying lunch-
eon in the embassy dining room, the chief deputy took the
problem for the first time to Jesus.

"Mr. Ambassador, if you have a moment?"

"Certainly, Peter. Sit down."

The older man edged carefully onto a teakwood chair beside the ambassador's desk. He sat with his legs clamped in a
vise before him.

"As you know, sir, in an isolated post like this, relations
between the younger men quite often become strained. In the
past I've not mentioned these problems because they were
minor and resolved as soon as they arose. With John the situation is different."

The ambassador smiled fondly, and Peter tightened the
pressure on his legs. "John is difficult," Jesus said.

"It's more than that, sir. He infuriates the other men."
Peter paused and for a moment let his knees swing free. "You
know, they all think very highly of you. To the staff, to all of
us, you are a man we deeply admire."

The ambassador still wore the smile that had greeted John's
name. "Thank you, Peter."

"It's for that reason that they resent John, sir. He tells them
that they don't appreciate you. He tells them—"

"Yes?"

"He tells them that he is the only one to understand your
complexity, that you are—if you will forgive me—not so fine
as you appear."

"He says that?"

"In fairness, he also says that, for the same reason, you are
even better than they realize."

"That is strange for him to say."

"The others find his attitude most galling—patronizing to
them and insulting to you. Several have threatened him, sir,
and others have talked of leaving—either a request for transfer
or quitting the service entirely."

"Drastic reactions."

"Emotions are intense here, sir—the surroundings, the delicacy of the mission."

"What do you recommend?"

"If I may be frank: a transfer for John. Perhaps to a larger station where he might have a wider scope of duties and associations."

"That's impossible."

Peter rose at the abrupt tone of the reply. "Failing that, sir, perhaps you could talk with him quite candidly about what I have told you. I don't know that his manner and attitude won't always serve to nettle his associates, but if he were to end at least his more obvious provocations—"

"I'm sorry, Peter. I can do nothing."

The older man nodded at once, as though the answer were not only one he wanted to hear but one he had helped to formulate.

"Don't accept my refusal in such good grace," Jesus said with a teasing smile. "Argue."

"No, sir."

"John would argue, and that's why I must have him. There's no pleasure in commanding, my dear friend, if there is no impertinence."

Peter never spoke before he thought, but this time he allowed himself to do both at once. "Whatever you may choose to call it, sir, I'm afraid the men see it as favoritism, and they consider it a form of weakness."

"Now," Jesus said in the chiding voice he had mastered so long before, "now, Peter, you're being impertinent."

Salve, salvation. Jesus asked himself, Have I confused the two? Is my name from Hoshea a mockery? Casting the words into other languages comforted him: *Unguento, salvación.*

pommade, *salvation*. We are so easily misled by labels. Whatever they are called, I am sure that a soft balm and God's blessing are nothing alike.

Beneath her eye paint and hair shellac, Mary Magdalene was a softer girl than she seemed to be. She lay on her couch and threw cashews to Jesus sitting cross-legged on the floor. "I've never taken any money for it," she said, licking the salt from a nut and from her fingers.

"No?"

"That's the truth. That really is. I've never taken a penny. Do you believe me?"

"Yes."

"Well, you should, because it's the truth. Well, there's another part to it, actually. I've never been offered any money either. That takes some of the glory out of it, doesn't it?"

Jesus had gorged himself on cashews, but he motioned for her to throw another. "We're not lucky enough to confront every temptation. Would you have taken money?"

"Sure."

"Toss me another one of those, will you? And then I'm not going to eat any more."

"There's something I don't understand." The tall young man had cleared his voice for the occasion.

"It's not about your name, is it, Tom Judas? I've explained that we need two of you so that men don't come to believe they can avoid a temptation by avoiding its name. You can't be Thomas any longer. You must redeem the name Judas from the dishonor of Iscariot."

"It's not about that."

"What, then?"

"I don't understand why simple people accept you so readily and the more learned men resist your message."

"Once I asked that question where I thought I would get the best answer. I was told that the simple people are unfailingly tolerant."

"That's not what I would have thought."

"There's one condition: They are tolerant if you live among them and accept them. Then they will accept you."

"Otherwise?"

"If you live apart, from choice or circumstance, they will fear you for your strangeness or hate you for the judgment you are making on them."

"And the more intelligent men?"

"Let's call them the less simple men. They can accept you when you are far away. In their midst, you must expect trouble."

"Which is better?"

"For a man, simple men. For an idea, the less simple men."

"So you prefer simple men."

"Is that what I said?"

The young man's throat had tightened again, and he cleared it with a slow gargle. "Then—"

"Judas," Jesus interrupted, "don't you think we had a better time wrangling over your new name?"

"Have I told you about the time I stole the money?" Jesus asked.

"I can't believe it."

"It's the truth. Something came over me—isn't that the expression? We had taken a collection after one of my more successful sermons."

"Which one?"

"I don't remember. Different generations seized on different messages. I thought they were all much the same."

"What happened?"

"We took in several thousand small bills. I tied them into a bundle and left."

"Why?"

"I was tired. The men weren't good, and that makes a difference. My mother was a scold, and you were forever whining. So I got on a train. I knew they'd make some excuse for me."

"Where did you go?"

"To the coast. It was mild there, and sunny and dry. I rented a room on the beach and slept soundly for a week."

"You felt guilty."

"I guess I did. I had no energy or taste for anything. I'd get up in the morning, walk a few yards along the ocean and be so tired I'd climb back in bed."

"What did you do with the money?"

"Nothing. I had never thought about it before, but it turned out that there wasn't anything I wanted. At night I'd decide to go out—have a good dinner, some entertainment. And I'd lie on my bed until it was too late and every place was closed."

"What a waste."

"Yes. I wouldn't mind having some of the money this time."

"What would you do with it?"

"I'd buy each of you something. A token. I've learned to understand the need you have for that kind of gift. Something to hold."

"That's—"

"What's wrong?"

"I've had too much wine. I'm sorry. I didn't mean—"

"Go ahead."

"I hate to have you see."

"I've seen people cry before, and they've seen me."

"I was going to be different."

"It's not important," Jesus said.

"Tell me what happened."

"One day, about two months later, I picked a newspaper out of the sand and read what I was supposed to have said the night before. I'd been replaced, it turned out, with no trouble at all. From that time on, I'd see articles and pictures of me quite often."

"And you on the beach—what were you?"

"I learned that I was a drunkard, living on the last of an uncle's inheritance."

"That's odd. You don't like liquor."

"None of us did, none of the men I used to meet every day at the bar. Until tonight, I'd forgotten that bar—no name outside, dirty dark wood walls, splintered chairs. And stained glass in one of the side windows."

"That was cruel."

"Don't underestimate God."

"Did you live long?"

"No, the whiskey did its job. I was broke at the end, and the state buried me at public expense."

"Then you actually got better treatment from the government by shirking your duty than by holding onto your beliefs?"

"You sound surprised."

Jesus removed the blotter from his desk so that, after he had destroyed the paper on which he was about to write, his words would leave no impression.

I hate them because they are ferrets and hyenas, [he wrote] ready to run and yap after anything they have not seen before. Those who pursue me, I would line up and walk through their ranks with a heavy blade, severing their hands from their arms and slashing their bellies to their groins.

I would spare no one. I would cut away their rancid sex and the fingers they have used to play those dripping tubes and holes. I would skim open the tops of their heads, trail my fingers through the soup of their brains and throw down the lid again, as workmen cover an open sewer.

I would jab the point of my knife into their navels, twisting until the cords came undone and they were no longer sewed into themselves.

I would slice away, for pigs to feed upon, their meaty joints and ripe inner thighs. When I was done, they would stand before me, all flesh cut away, their bones glistening through blood and scraps of skin, their skulls open and their clutching bowels ready finally to receive. Then I could love them. My God, how I could love them then.

Jesus laid aside his pen and began to tear the sheet of paper into small pieces. Some men feel that way, he told himself, and perhaps I know them better for trying to play their part. For me it was nothing but an exercise. I don't want to mutilate or murder.

But why, as I wrote, did old wounds begin exciting me?

"What about the time you drove money-changers from the temple?"

Jesus looked into the face that loved him. "It was a lie."

"It didn't happen?"

"Nothing like it. I wasn't always sure of my fate, and I told many lies, most of them more important than that one."

"I don't care."

"You're right. Now I could do it, and it would be nothing for me. But when I told of it first, it was an act of courage to lie. Don't despise lies. They give us our best idea of what we are trying to become."

"Could you lie now?"

"No, our last words shouldn't be lies."

"Don't say that."

"All right: We will go on like this forever."

"Is that a lie?"

"A very common one."

Jesus decided that people were becoming much too rude. "Young lady," he said to a salesgirl, "you should not be so unpleasant."

"What?" she demanded. "What did you say to me?"

"Your behavior to that last customer was inexcusable. It doesn't concern me, because I will not be coming this way again. But for you rudeness has become a habit, and it will cause you much unhappiness."

"People are rude to me first," the girl said. "Almost all of them are. I have to be ready for it."

"You can't guide your life by the behavior of others. Forget everyone else. Be polite for your sake."

Her dull eyes lit with cunning. "I wonder how the idea got around that you were a nice guy. You don't care about anybody else, do you? Just yourself."

"You must choose whether you want to care about people or be good to them."

"You can't do both? You can't love people and always be kind to them?"

"No."

"Then maybe I'll go on being rude." She wheeled around

to grab an ashtray away from a woman at the counter. "Don't handle those! Don't you see the sign?"

She came back to Jesus and asked, "How was that?" But he had walked to another department.

Again Jesus had been perfect. When again the call did not come, he waited out his life patiently. Not for a minute did he regret his observance of every rule; but he puzzled over possible reasons that his perfection had not been crowned.

What have I lost by being exempt from one of man's great needs? How much do I ask of men that I would waive if I shared the full pressure of their bodies? When I learned to love my disciples, I became less harsh to the men who could not help putting their families before God. Would I subvert more commandments if I were burdened with sex?

I remind myself that God bestowed sex upon them for reasons men seldom understand. Reproduction was the least consideration. A man could as easily have created children with a movement of his bowels. But sex was to be the way for him to burst his skin and flood another body with liquid from the center of his being.

They were given this way to touch and reach so that the emptiest men and the most forlorn could find their way without thought or words. I did not need their kind of communication; without stretching my hand, I could touch any one of them. Without condensing to fluid, my spirit could pass into other bodies. Sex was unnecessary for me, and I was made without it.

What have I lost? Not the ability to understand a deep

and final union. The harmony of a good marriage comes at
least within my range.

But what of the lost and lonely? My mind grasps their
despair. I understand that a woman lying in bed alone can
freeze between her legs. I know that a man can be bent from
the unrelieved weight in his wrinkled lumps of flesh. When
they do not meet, that man and woman, I know their need
can corrode and kill them.

Knowing is not feeling. I understand their desperation, and
I have stayed a priest's hand raised against a prostitute. But
the other misuses of their sex I have attacked with righteousness and ignorance. If ever again I am made sure about my
message and myself, I will ask to be given that one last link
with mankind. I will see if, with it, I can remain the Son
of God.

God swept in while Christ was lost in daydreams. "Finished?" he asked peremptorily.

"Almost."

"You should be done by this time. I've told you it doesn't
pay to hesitate. What have you got left—the floods?"

Christ spun the earth idly. "No, I put one there," he
touched the globe, "and another up there."

"That looks all right." When he could do it honestly, God
liked to sound encouraging. To himself, he wondered whether
Christ would ever learn to work with speed and efficiency.
To stir a harmless competition, he said, "Lambda has been
done for hours."

"Lambda works with dust." Christ spoke indifferently.

"It means a great deal to him. He's spent time among
those particles. In his way, he loves them, and his job is no
easier than yours."

"I'm sorry."

"Why don't you finish quickly and join the others? What's holding you back today?"

"A broken spine."

"Is that all? Assign it now and come along with me. Do you have the list?"

He snatched a paper from Christ's hand and read through it rapidly. "A good distribution on fires. I don't think I could have done as well." God moved his finger down the list again. "Here he is," he said. "Here's the man for the back." He shoved the paper back to Christ.

"Yes, I've seen his name."

"Then what is the delay?"

Christ spun the globe slowly between his knees and watched blurs of green and blue and occasional spots of yellow roll past his forefinger.

"If they didn't handle murder and war for themselves," God said reproachfully, "we'd have to get you a helper."

"I've heard from that man's wife," Christ said at last. "She calls every night."

"What does she want?"

"She doesn't want anything. She loves her husband and her family, and she calls to thank me for them. I've come to look forward to hearing from her. Even on busy nights she manages to get through."

God had begun paging through the book he carried everywhere. Its plain black cover was battered and some pages were dog-eared and stained. As a gift, they had presented him one year with a volume bound in green Florentine leather and indexed in gold. God had said the new book was far too handsome to use in his everyday work, and he had put it aside for some important occasion.

"Here they are," God said. "Married twenty-two years. Husband sustained minor wounds in a war. Son studying to be an engineer. Daughter with a minor talent for water colors." He slapped the book shut and confronted Christ. "Why

shouldn't she give thanks?" he demanded. "What have they
had to bear but his small nick in the shoulder and two cases
of mumps?" He riffled through the pages of his book. "How
many do you find like them?"

Defiantly Christ said, "Not enough."

"Not enough to make people slothful and weak," God said.
"Not enough so that they forget how to handle adversity and
death. How often I've told you, and how little you remember: I don't apportion sickness and storms because I enjoy
their suffering. I don't do it to test their faith. I know the
depth of a human being's faith, and I find no need to depress
myself with new demonstrations."

"I remember that my performance depressed you."

"You were sent as a man. I didn't expect anything else.
But these men and women of yours are going to die, and they
have to be prepared for it. Can you imagine a life in which
they passed from pleasure to pleasure, never failing in mind
or body, until they were suddenly taken away. We must convince them of death's blessings, and sickness has proved to be
our most persuasive argument."

"Must they die?"

God's anger never failed to intimidate Christ. "We'll let
them live again as we once did," he said bitterly. "Two hundred, three hundred, five hundred years—until they come to
hate the patterns of their lives and until the weight of repe-
tition crushes them and until they choose death by the millions. We'll let you explain to them then why they had to
keep on living after their will had gone and after breathing,
the mere taking in of air, had become boring beyond their
endurance."

"I forgot how it was."

"Look at you! Look at your own choice! Whenever you
can, you hurry back here while your body is young and strong.
You don't wait until age rots out your belly and shrivels your
skin. One gray hair on your chest and you're back, away from
the very people who are causing you such anguish today."

Christ nodded.

"They understand their fate better than you do," God continued. "Your miracles have become an embarrassment to them. They know they must bear the suffering they've been allotted, but they've become confused: to make you happy should they journey off to a cave and pray for health? Should they do that to prove their faith? Or should they stay at home, as their instincts tell them, and learn to live and die with their afflictions? You've muddled their thinking. I warned you, but your foolish sympathies led you astray."

"The healing was a mistake," Christ granted.

In a more kindly way, God said, "There's no point in going over all that again. Finish up now and meet me with the others."

"All right."

"If that woman doesn't call tonight, don't worry," God added as he was about to leave. "They'll be busy with him at the hospital. Then a shock sets in, and it might be a week or more. But from what you say, she'll get along. They're tougher than you remember."

When he had gone, Christ turned resolutely to the globe, checked coordinates and moved his marker to a microscopic dot in the middle of a continent. One jab, and he could cross the broken back off his day's list and hurry to join the others in the lounge.

That night Christ was sitting by the switchboard with a receiver in his hand when he heard the flat soft voice begin to speak. "I don't believe," she said, and even with the poor connection, Christ could hear her sniffle, "that we have the right to ask for health or money or happiness. Tom might not agree with me. You know he's never done much praying, and when he comes out of the anesthetic tonight, he might ask you for an end to his pain. You know what suffering can do to even a brave man.

"I'm not asking for courage either. If I can do my part while he's in the hospital, it's because you gave me the strength long ago, and it's been inside me waiting to be used.

"Tonight I want only to thank you, as I have every other night, for giving me a man to love and children to take care of. This day was bad for us, but we have had many wonderful days, and I thank you as much for today as for any of the others."

Her voice faded, and Christ put down the receiver. The equipment had been built without speakers, and his answer to her stayed unspoken. "Don't take this," he would have said. "There was no cause. There was no reason. And whatever you do, don't thank me. You cannot offer thanks. I won't let you."

God found him sitting by the switchboard and put an arm around his shoulder. "I suppose she didn't call."

Christ looked at him through red-rimmed eyes. "She called," he said furiously. "She called and she cursed us both. She hates you. She said she will never forgive you."

To Christ, God's smile looked hideous. "She will, though. She'll forgive me. You both will."

A brazen girl possessed of seven devils was brought before Jesus to be cured. "I am going to cast out those seven devils from you," he said.

"May I ask you for a favor?" She spoke impudently.

"What is it?"

"Cast out six."

His answers to his questions:

Q. Why do you give?

A. I'm too selfish to take.

Q. Why do you preach?
A. I'm too lazy to listen.
Q. Why do you go on?
A. I'm too tired to stop.

Christ was exhausted, and he would have preferred to lie in the tomb for another twenty-four hours. The dampness in the air had not penetrated the skins in which he had been wrapped, and a pile of furs made the floor of the cave warm and soft. But when the time had come, he pulled back the wrappings and braced himself for a rush of cold air. Instead, the tomb itself seemed snug and dry. Pulling his robes around him, he saw that he had been dressed in fresh linen richly embroidered with green vines and leaves. This luxury could neither clear his head nor ease the aching in his shoulders. As he drew near the stone over the cave's mouth, he groaned softly to himself.

A prolonged wait often faced him before the boulder could be removed. Today he had barely reached the entrance when the stone rolled an inch, enough to let in a crack of light that hurt his eyes. At the same time he thought he heard music— not the disembodied strings that sometimes welcomed him, but a full-bodied band playing an army march. As the stone rolled further, the music was lost beneath a chorus of cheers and shouts. And when the mouth of the cave was uncovered, Christ saw thousands of people before him, crying his name and throwing into the air banners of silk and bright spring flowers.

The glare of the sun and the din of the crowd drove him back into the cave, where he was joined by a beaming giant he recognized as the dour Peter. "What is this?" Christ asked weakly.

"A celebration, Lord, to mark your resurrection." The huge man was hopping with excitement.

"We usually do this more privately."

"In the past, yes. But now there's no need. We shall never be secretive again. No midnight flights, no coded messages, no trips through back pathways and deserted alleys. We are here now to take you through the main gate and down the widest avenues of the city. Everyone in Jerusalem is waiting along the streets, and there isn't a flower left unplucked in the kingdom."

"What!" Christ exclaimed. "Who do these people think I am?"

"Why, Jesus, the risen Christ!" Peter's cry, echoing in the cave, set off another chorus of cheers from the throng.

Christ gripped his head. "Please."

Peter stepped before the people and made the smallest motion with one finger. At once they were so silent that Christ looked up to see if they had disappeared. Thousands of happy faces smiled at him and began to turn red. "They must breathe, after all," Christ said, and Peter made another motion. A mass exhalation swept past them.

"Explain this to me," Christ demanded sternly. He did not like jokes.

"I cannot explain it, Lord. I can but tell you what has happened."

"Tell me."

"On the day you were taken from the cross—"

"Friday. The day before yesterday."

"Yes. As we put you in the tomb, not only our grief but our outrage was profound. We wanted to tell everyone, everyone all at once, what a shameful act had been committed that day. We started with the people who had gathered around the tomb—the idle and curious, expecting them to ridicule us and scorn your dead body. Instead of that, they believed. They accepted immediately everything we taught, and they ran to tell others. All doubts faded, and the circle of faith spread and widened throughout the night and all day Saturday. By this morning not a man lived on the face of the earth who did not accept your divinity. Everyone worships you."

"Not everyone," Christ said with confidence. "Maybe a large number, an unprecedented following. But not everyone."

"Everyone," Peter repeated obstinately.

"Not Herod."

At the sound of his name, the king came forward, his arm around Philip's neck. He looked shrunken without his jeweled crown, and the coarse sacking of his tan robe ended above his knees. "I hope you can forgive me as our father has," Herod said from a kneeling posture.

"Get him to his feet," Christ said uncomfortably. He helped to jerk on the king's thin elbow until he was looking again into the small regal eyes. "Where are your velvet robes?"

"What need have I with velvet when I have been wrapped in God's infinite mercy?"

Christ motioned Peter to one side. "You must be careful," he said. "I think he's plotting something."

Peter fell back in astonishment. "Oh, no, Lord! The depth of his new faith has been an inspiration to us all. Only Caesar has been more eloquent in describing his conversion."

"Caesar is not here?" Christ, who felt uneasy with men of temporal power, was faintly alarmed.

"No, we have asked him to stay in Rome as an example to the citizens there. We were afraid everyone in the world would rush to Jerusalem and the surface of the earth would collapse."

"Very wise."

"Caesar wants you to come to Rome to assume his duties, but we were not sure an emperor would be needed with the day of judgment so near."

"Judgment."

"The fact that the end of the world is imminent impressed

many of our converts mightily. Between us," Peter lowered his voice to an urgent whisper, "how soon do you think it will be?"

"We can discuss it later," Christ said. "I'm tired now, and I'd like to go to my mother's house."

Peter's radiance was glowing ever brighter. "We have no houses, Lord," he said proudly. "Every building in the village was burned last night."

"Vandals?"

"Priests! We remembered your counsel: 'You cannot serve God and Mammon' and 'Do not lay up for yourselves treasures on earth.' We saw that homes were a form of treasure, so we razed them throughout the night and stand before you now as lilies."

"Yes," Christ said. "Is my mother here?"

"Bring forth Mary, mother of God," Peter called, provoking a fresh hail of blossoms.

Mary appeared, her normally apologetic mouth and imploring eyes lit with new confidence. In the past Christ had resented her because he thought she looked on him more as a son than a savior. "Hello, Mother."

"Greetings, Lord." Although the words were impeccable, her manner suggested a certain jaunty equality.

"I am happy to see you," he heard himself saying. His head still ached and conversation came painfully.

"We're getting along well."

"I thought I would join you for dinner. I'm not feeling strong, and I think a good meal might help me."

"Open your hand," Mary said briskly. When he had done as she said, she scooped a mound of berries from her pocket and poured them into his palm. "There."

"What are these?" He rolled the dried black fruit over his palm. They were too shriveled and hard to leave a stain.

"Dinner," she said. "We aren't killing animals or fish any more."

"I have never forbidden the eating of meats."

"I know, Lord. You were a hearty eater, but no one blames you for that."

"Blames me?" Christ shouted until his head rocked. "Blames me?"

Mary took his hand and led him back to the pile of furs. "Everyone realizes that you had to make some compromises because of the way the world was then. But the world has changed, and you don't have to cloak your words or equivocate any longer. You can be yourself in all your inspired goodness. We are ready for you."

"I see."

"Now you must come out and greet the crowds. Each man wants to share with you his own story of redemption and abiding faith."

"I don't feel—"

"They've been waiting so patiently," Mary said. "Some of them wanted to come for you yesterday to tell you the good news, but we decided to wait until word came back from Gaul and we knew the conversions were one hundred percent."

Christ rose from the bed and followed her outside. As he reached the throng, however, the eager men and glowing women saw that he was pale and trembling from exhaustion. They stepped back to make a passage for him, letting their broad smiles and the sympathetic crinkling of their eyes speak for them.

When Christ had passed to the fringes of the crowd, he came upon a row of donkeys, each carrying an enormous basket of coins. "What a fine offering!" Christ exclaimed, running his fingers through the silver, copper and gold. "We shall be able to do great good among the poor."

"No, Lord!" Peter answered with some agitation. "We are sending that caravan to the Dead Sea, where all the coins of Palestine will be pushed to the bottom. The jewels we are taking to the ocean, for fear their sparkle on the sea's depth might distract us from the wonders of God's world."

"You are casting away all that money?"

"It is easier for a camel to go through the eye of a needle than for a rich man to enter the kingdom of God," Peter quoted sonorously.

"Do you believe the crews will actually dispose of their loads? They will hide the money away for their own use."

Peter's mouth worked anxiously. "Lord," he said, "those days are past. We don't need to probe and doubt and question any more. You will find that you need no longer seek proof of devotion on every side. Your former entreaties for evidence of faith, your challenges that we found so painful, they can be laid aside at last. The men in charge of the money and jewels don't want to hide anything for themselves. They want to remove a source of corruption from the world, and then they want to obey your every instruction. We don't question each other's sincerity or devise tests to torment ourselves. We don't need to."

"You make me very happy." Christ was trying to say something more spirited when his attention was drawn to a commotion near a lemon grove. They could hear a man's young voice heavy with indignation. "Apparently there are still some injustices that need correcting," Christ said. Peter looked up sharply at his tone.

"That's Stephen," he replied. "He's full of the holy spirit."

They joined the crowd that had surrounded a man with a full blond beard and bright brown eyes. Next to him cowered a middle-aged farmer, his robe and boots thick with soil and manure. "I'm sorry," the man kept repeating, "I'm sorry, I'm sorry."

"He probably stole a sheep," Christ said cheerfully, "but he seems well on the way to repentance."

"No, Lord," Peter corrected him. "I recognize that man now. He had devised a new implement that he claimed made plowing easier. Stephen, of course, told him to destroy the tool and gave him wise instruction throughout the night. The man saw that he had only hoped to make himself esteemed and honored before his fellows, and he was overcome with shame at his baseness. He insisted that Stephen reveal to the multitude the enormity of his offense and the justice of Stephen's castigation."

"If it made the work easier—"

"But at what cost! Are we to introduce again pride, envy and that unworthy struggle for mankind's good opinion? Besides, the world will soon end, and our plowing and harvesting will be over."

"Certainly."

They wandered further through the city, Christ accepting with raised hand the tributes of the population. He addressed the Parthians and Medes, Elamites and Mesopotamians, Judeans and Cappadocians, each in his own language. He spoke also Phrygian and Pamphylian, not unwilling to demonstrate the talents bestowed on him by resurrection, and he extended words of greeting as well in Egyptian, Latin and Arabic. Only one Libyan student, his eyes filled with love, saw fit to stop Christ respectfully and correct his pronunciation.

After a time, Christ motioned to Peter before they approached the next throng. "I am scarcely contributing to their faith or future," he complained.

"It's all they ask—that you be with them."

"That's not enough," Christ said firmly. "Bring the sick and afflicted to me."

Overhearing his call, an old man, lame in a leg and blind in one eye, hobbled forward. "Do you have a task for me, Master?"

"I am going to heal you."

Fear in his good eye, the man backed hastily away. "Oh, don't! Don't!" he cried. "Peter, make him stop!"

"Do not be alarmed." Turning to his disciples, Christ tried to sound more gentle. "What troubles him?"

"He believes that he was persecuted for righteousness' sake. The night after you had driven money-lenders from the temple, he set fire to a banker's house. The police broke his leg and put out his eye. Of course the officers who did it have repented fully and begged forgiveness. But this man remembers your words."

"Which words?"

" 'Theirs is the kingdom of heaven.' " The cripple had drawn closer. "That's what you told us. Now that it's almost mine, you want to heal me. How could I ever prove on judgment day that I was persecuted for righteousness' sake?"

Peter took the man lovingly by the shoulder. "If Christ wants to cure you—"

The old man started to weep. "I was being selfish," he sobbed. "If he wants to cure me, there is good reason. I am ready to give up the kingdom of heaven, if that is Christ's will. Let him mend my leg. Oh, Lord, forgive my lapse in faith! Heal my eye even, if that is your wish." He was convulsed with shame. "Anything! Anything! Make me young!" His words were becoming frenzied. "Make me handsome! Make me rich! Punish me any way you like!"

"Let us move on." Christ turned toward a group of radiant young matrons. "Hello, Master." A pretty girl, not yet twenty, curtsied as Christ approached.

Christ asked amiably, "What is your name?"

"Rachel, Lord." She had a thin face with large brown eyes and a finely molded nose.

"When did the word of God reach you, Rachel?"

"Yesterday, Lord. My mother came with the word as I nursed my baby."

"A baby?" Christ heard himself lapse into an avuncular manner he detested. "Where is the little one?"

Rachel looked surprised. "I don't know. Home, I suppose."

"You don't know? Who is looking after it?"

"I don't know. No one. When I heard that you were risen,

I came here at once." She saw the look on Christ's face and turned to Peter for support. "That was right, wasn't it? I was right to come? 'He who loves son or daughter more than me is—' "

" 'Not worthy of me,' " Christ concluded wearily. "Which is it?"

"What?"

"Son or daughter?"

"Oh, daughter," she said indifferently. "Two months old."

"You were right to come," Peter spoke reassuringly. "But perhaps it's time to return now."

"I'd like to stay. To follow Christ."

"He must be leaving soon. He appreciates your devotion, but he cannot stay much longer now."

"That's right," Christ said.

"I live five miles from here," the girl answered. "To the north. I hope you will be passing our house soon. I'll have cold water waiting for you. None of us will drink our water from the well. We'll save it for you."

"Of course, if the baby—" Christ began.

"The baby!" she scoffed.

"What do you call her?"

"I changed the name yesterday to Mary. All the mothers did. We're calling all our babies Mary."

"Not the boys?"

She giggled. "No, they are all named for you."

"We were afraid it might be confusing," Peter explained, "but since the end is so near, no real objection seemed in order."

"No."

They walked a little longer, Peter tugging at his sleeve now and then to point out especially noteworthy examples of conversion. "There is no exception," Christ acknowledged. "They are all saved."

"They are all saved," Peter confirmed. "Ah, here is Stephen.

Isn't he a fine man, Lord? Although, of course, Timon is also splendid, and the other five new recruits are of the highest caliber despite the fact that their mettle will never be tested."

"Who is Timon?"

"We did not encounter him, Lord. I believe he is touring the southern provinces. But he is magnificent—very young, unusually quick-witted and single-minded in his devotion." Peter paused to greet Stephen. "I was telling the risen Christ about the brilliance of our young friend Timon."

"A fine boy." Stephen's agreement was so prompt and complete that it ended the conversation. Christ studied him carefully and found what he sought in the set of Stephen's jaw.

"I'm off to bed." Christ looked gratefully again at Stephen's face. "I know that your efforts here have freed me of further labors, and I'm not sure what more I can contribute. But in the morning I may find something to occupy me."

Why must Judas always look the same? The others change with the age and circumstance. Peter's ugliness can be imposing or endearing, and James's attractiveness sometimes lies in his glowing darkness and sometimes in his fair transparency.

Only Judas never changes. He is forever thin, with eyes that are moist and a large nose damper still. Why couldn't he, for once, be squat and swarthy with polished nails? Or at least without those pores that open like a hundred mouths across his chin? Or stocky and blond, a farmer? Or a merchant wrapped in a spirit as tightly rolled as his umbrella?

Instead, Judas is the man who needs me most and, always, the one I can least help. He comes to me reeking of hopes and desires, and I hear him telling me with every grimace and shrug, every misplaced familiarity and every wince at imaginary wounds, that he comes more as a patient than as a disciple.

He stands there, daring me to cure him, and he never stops saying, "Hate me, revile me, don't make me love you by letting me near you. Help me keep my icy bitterness at my heart without your breath to melt it. Help me multiply my hatreds until their taste chokes my throat."

I grant his lesser wish. The love he craves, the love he fears, he does not get from me. I betray Judas as he demands of me. We both know that is our story, no matter how it is later told by men who are blind to love. Mine is the betrayal.

Girding himself for Earth, the newest Jesus had decided to acquire a knowledge of mathematics. "Do you know," he asked Christ one day, "how many grains of sand it would take to fill up the universe?"

"One."

The Jesus was confused and cross. "No, it would take ten to the hundredth power. That's one oh oh oh—" Counting on his fingers, he repeated the "oh" for a full minute. When he had finished, he drew a breath and said, "How could you say one?"

Christ said, "We'll talk about it when you get back."

The guard stood six or seven inches taller than Jesus, and because Jesus was his prisoner, he looked even taller than that. His chest threatened to burst the seams of his khaki blouse, and his thighs looked swollen too, but healthier and harder. His blond hair had been clipped so short that the top of his head shone as red as his cheeks. Short and upturned, the guard's nose was the standard nose among his countrymen. "They can't help looking like pigs," Peter had once said to Jesus. "But they can help acting like them."

"We will enter here for interrogation." He pulled Jesus to a halt beside an open door. Although the guard's inflection was good, Jesus replied, "It may be easier for you if we speak your language."

"As you wish. I would not want you to say later that you had misunderstood what you signed."

"Why would I say that?"

The guard spoke offhandedly. "Men sometimes repudiate the statements they make here. It's not surprising. There are even men who break their marriage vows."

"My word is good."

"No doubt."

The room had one pine table and two chairs, all uncomfortably low. Seated, Jesus felt as though he were squatting, and the table top was hardly higher than his ankles.

"We will fill out the forms rapidly," the guard said. "I know you have not had much sleep." From a drawer in the low table, he brought out a long green form. "Name?"

"Jesus of Nazareth."

Irony glinted like a monocle in the guard's eye. "I'm afraid I'll need your real name."

"That is my name."

"No doubt. But I meant the name you were born with."

"I don't remember. It's not significant."

The faint smile faded from the guard's full mouth. "It may not be significant to the Son of God," he said harshly. "But for mortals trying to keep accurate prison records, it is essential."

"I'm sorry." Jesus spoke contritely as he ransacked his memory. "I keep thinking it was short and guttural, but that was another time. I don't remember."

"Some of us, less favored by the Almighty, manage nevertheless to remember our own names."

"I've told you my name. What you are asking for is little

different from a play word that a child might make up during an afternoon of pretending."

The guard wrote on the top line, "Jesus, son of Joseph." He said, "When you put it that way, I can't blame you. As you spoke, I tried to remember a name I had used one weekend last month at a hotel in the country. I've already forgotten. But in other respects that weekend remains very vivid in my mind."

Jesus hoped he would not begin to talk about his success with women; people often wanted to confide that part of their lives to him. Telling about his adventures, the guard might relax for a moment, but later he would punish Jesus for his own indiscretion.

It was to ward off reminiscences that Jesus volunteered, "My age is thirty-five."

"I am two years younger," the guard answered. "But look how much older I seem to be. You act young for your age."

"I don't feel young."

The guard threw out his chest as though displaying a host of medals. "I don't mean that I look old. I am talking about bearing and manner, the authority that military command gives to a man. You have none of that."

"I haven't bothered for a long time," Jesus said. "You end up impressing the wrong people, or yourself."

"There is nothing wrong with standing straight, with squaring your shoulders and planting your two feet solidly on the ground and saying deep from your gut that you are a man."

"I have seen men on their knees as they made the same confession."

"It is a boast."

"We will not agree," Jesus said mildly. "My occupation— if you wish to continue with the form—was peddling. I sold small items from a handcart."

"While preaching sedition."

"Did I?"

"Don't be alarmed. That wasn't why you were arrested. Our intelligence office found your efforts laughable."

"Women coming to buy shoelaces or paring knives would ask me questions, and I would answer. Toward the end, they were bringing their children and their husbands. It was bad for business." Jesus smiled. "I was talking more than I was selling."

"You are a talkative man, after all."

Jesus nodded his head, almost a shrug, and blinked deprecatingly. "I had been silent for years. I see now that during that time I was preparing answers. When people asked me questions, I could reply without a pause. If I had hesitated, they might have lost interest and left. Instead, my answers became a habit for them. They came to depend too much on me."

"What sort of thing did they ask?"

"At the last, they wanted to know if they should turn over strangers to your army in order to save their own husbands and parents. It was a question I hated."

The guard seemed scarcely interested in his story, and Jesus wondered whether that was a method of extracting information—to appear indifferent while at the same time making notes to be used at a trial. Except for the guard's sake, Jesus told himself, I do not care if he has been chosen to betray me.

"You hated to make that decision for them," the guard said sympathetically.

"It wasn't that. If I had been of any value to them during the previous years, they would never have asked the question."

"That's right." The guard sat forward as though playing a card he had almost overlooked. "You're Jesus of Nazareth. The problems that torment other people are very simple to you."

"Except remembering my name." Jesus was not ashamed to

make a joke at his own expense. Peter thought it was an unworthy device, but sometimes it had changed the course of a dispute and brought antagonists into their ranks.

"I am not Jesus of Nazareth," the guard said.

"No."

"So I would not betray my family for a cause or a future reward or even to save strangers across the city. I respect life and I serve my country. But I love only a few people, and I would do anything in the world to protect them."

"They were asking what I would do, not what they should do."

The guard had laid aside his pen. A corner of the interrogation form was wrinkling under his elbow, and Jesus, who loved order, wanted to reach across the table to straighten the paper before it became creased.

"That's a convenient confusion to foster, isn't it?" the guard was asking. "When the age for preaching passes, switch instead to self-effacement. But the impossible standards remain, the guilt remains."

"Guilt?"

"The guilt you have managed to breed in any man or woman or child fool enough to give you a hearing. The guilt and sense of failure that you've raised to a level of perfection that has never been matched. You've found a way to strike at even the best men—if they live a blameless life, you condemn them for their thoughts. It was your God that shackled men to their lusts. Then, knowing they couldn't change, you came to demand that they free themselves. You examined the nature God gave men and called it base, but you made your complaints to men, not to God. Once you praised the lilies of the field. But if a man manages to live as he has been formed to live, you threaten him with eternal fire."

The length and vehemence of the guard's outburst astonished Jesus. He was the more disturbed because the man's voice had gradually dropped as he continued. At the end, his scorn seemed to have turned to sorrow. Jesus was not used to men speaking to him with pity in their voices.

"Do I hurt you so much?"

"You can't hurt me at all." The guard took up the paper as though to proceed, but his eyes were not focused on it. "Only what you believe can hurt you, and I haven't believed your lies since I was a boy."

"What made you stop?"

"It became a matter of survival." The guard had regained enough composure to tilt back on his low chair and stare beyond the doorway as though he could watch his childhood staged again. "I had to make a choice: either you and death or me and life. With the innocence—ignorance—of a twelve-year-old, I'd tried to meet your every standard. Of course, one by one I failed your tests. I couldn't control my thoughts about the girls on the street. I couldn't learn to love all the boys who bullied me. I could not, with my whole heart, believe in your God. At our church, the pastor listened patiently to these confessions. He said that as long as I knew my thoughts were wrong, as long as I tried my best to forgive, as long as I believed in God's existence more than I doubted, then I was following on your path. But I knew better than to compromise. Youth always knows better, and that's why the young are so unhappy. I knew what you had taught, and I knew how miserably I had failed. I got ready to kill myself."

Jesus said nothing and searched the face of the guard for a boy who had suffered.

The guard took his silence for argument. "Do you think I was the first child to hate himself in your name? If so, you've succeeded very well in shutting yourself off from the world."

"I've often been surrounded by children who loved me." The guard had disturbed Jesus, and he put forward his objection tentatively.

"No doubt weak and ordinary children fight for your favor,

They want to have the ball thrown out of reach, not so they must jump higher but so no one can condemn them for falling short."

"I had thought weak men wanted low standards."

"For them the standard is never low enough. Only a God demanding the impossible can reconcile them to their failings."

"I've thought of men as men," Jesus said. "I've spoken sometimes of distinctions among them, but I believed their similarity outweighed any differences."

The guard smiled ruefully. "You've lost none of your skill for reaching out carelessly and striking the sorest spot. Of course I have to admit to what you say: I am a man with all the weaknesses that the species has inherited. But my boast is that I am a strong specimen of a weak species, and I found my strength on the day I killed you in my heart. That day I began to let myself live."

"I have heard these arguments advanced by philosophers," Jesus said, "but unless a man has lived by his philosophy, I've not been interested. You seem to be telling me a lesson from your life. I will try to answer you."

"It's too late."

"For you. Not for me."

The guard looked out to the hall that led to rows of cells. "For you."

"You're saying that I will die soon? I knew that before I was brought here. Until you have to turn me over to the killers of your state, let me answer you."

"You have nothing to tell me."

"Let me understand your accusation: I asked more from you than you could give? I made you feel you had failed in the eyes of God? If that's your complaint, you're not afraid of me. You fear the truth. Certainly you and every other man has failed in the eyes of God. Will you learn to raise yourself above your failure? Or will you try to blind God by blinding yourself? I would think that for a man—since that title pleases you—the choice would not be hard."

"The choice was even easier than you make it. I broke out of your prison. I, a boy who had hated the world and everything in it, learned to love nature—the nature in myself and the nature that surrounded me."

"What does this nature demand of you?"

"I make my own demands. I took a wife and gave her children. I fulfill my duty to my country. Whenever I am drawn to other women I win them honestly and shamelessly. Shamelessly—that is a good word, just one of the words you tried to ruin for us. I feed and clothe my family, and I teach the children about the world as it is. Someday I'll die. But until I do, the palms of my hands, the insides of my ears, the hairs on my belly itch and prickle with life."

Jesus could not boast that kind of vitality, though in patience and strength he surpassed other men. Anyone who felt the blood pound in his veins awed him a little. "That life you're holding in your palm," Jesus said, "slips each hour through your fingers."

"Let it go! At least I don't clasp my hands in prayer, trying to trap immortality as a child catches butterflies. My fingers have been in many places where I was happy to leave a part of my life."

"If you have found a pattern that suits you, why hate me?"

The guard breathed deeply before he answered. He seemed to take in more air than he exhaled. "Because you still have hold of me by the ankles and the ears. Before my body grew out of your control, you laid your hands on me, and I have never got completely away. I can writhe and twist my trunk— that part of me I can move freely. But I can never leap as high as I would like because your hands are a chain at my feet. I can never turn my head to see everything around me because you tweak my ears. You couldn't stunt me. I outgrew you. But I can't shake you loose."

"I've interfered with your pleasures?"

The guard clicked at his front teeth with a pencil, a sharp sound in the quiet room. "You would imagine that, no doubt, you poor eunuch. No doubt you're delighted when you can ruin the natural coupling of a man and woman. That's not where I feel your touch. You don't reach between my legs to pinch my pleasure. You interfere with my pain. That's why I can't forgive you."

"I thought I had added to your pain."

For a moment the guard seemed about to start again on the routine questioning. He seemed ready to look at Jesus out of blank eyes and to deny with his efficiency that he had revealed anything of himself. He had almost fallen into that impersonation when he coughed and stretched backward in his chair. "I believe in nothing you teach," he said. "I know that only emptiness surrounds me, and that when I die the void will claim me. I know and accept that. But deep in my wretched memory your lying promises have lodged themselves, and as I prepare myself each day for death, your words seduce my arguments. In some weak corner of my brain, I think: Perhaps I will be spared. And all your false hopes flood over me again. Even when I have reached to the bedrock of my being and I am looking into my life as a curator would, sorting and cataloguing fact from my fancy, I find your faith sticking to my fingertips. I can't put down your false hopes, and I realize then that you have perverted me in the worst way. You have smeared my truth with your mad faith."

"Why do you say mad?"

"I hate you least when I persuade myself that you're insane."

Jesus was never candid about his shortcomings. Yet he felt he must say, "Many men have had more powerful minds than mine. But I have never been insane."

By the time he answered, the guard spoke as though Jesus were a patient in their joint care. "What first alerted me was your prediction that the world would end soon after your death. In those days when I was tormented, I had hoped, even prayed, that the world could be destroyed at the precise moment that I chose to leave it. But when I became happy with my life, all that changed. Now I want people to enjoy this earth forever. I like to think of them lying on river banks, drinking wine all night and making love until the sunrise. I have come to see that through their lives I will live on. Only a madman wants to bring the world down around him."

"It was not my wish. It was God's will."

"Yet the world did not end. We have learned much in recent years from the Jews about the way men try to make their secret dreams come true. You confused your envy with God's judgment. But men live despite you, and soon men will live without you."

"You admit your indebtedness to those Jews?"

"They helped me rid myself of you. Our country, after all, has never said that Jews were not clever." The guard paused. "That was a diversion on your part, wasn't it? That was a way of shifting my attention to a political problem about which I am only slightly concerned and you care nothing at all. You have been restless, I think, since I first mentioned insanity."

Jesus said, "I will tell you all that I know: The prospect of insanity has troubled me more than anything else in my life. At God's command, I have been set apart from other men. But all the grace I feel, all the glory that passes through me, would be unbearable if I were mad." He stopped twisting his hands and clasped them to the wooden arms of his low chair.

"I have told myself," Jesus said, "that God could use a madman for my task. Nothing in that choice would be out of keeping with God's purpose. He could send dwarfs or drunkards. It was God who insisted I practice a humble trade when he could as easily have made me a prince. Surely I could carry out my duties if I were mad. But for me something would be lost. I would be dependent on men's sufferance, and they would give it. Men are kind when it costs them nothing. But I would lose too much. Even when I have failed, I have never shamed God. I've obeyed his orders to the end, and I have died for God. But I have died sane. To be less than sane, I would be an object. I would be no different from bushes made to burn or loaves made to multiply."

"You are forever out of step with your time," the guard said less harshly. "In Jerusalem you were killed as a mad Christ. Here you will die as a sane Jew."

"The Romans thought I threatened their government."

"We know better. We know your doctrine is an asset to our state."

"So I am to be killed as a Jew." Jesus thought of the thousands of men who had preceded him into the death chambers. "Then I have failed."

"Even death must be on your terms?"

"My life follows a formula. In this age of science that's become hard somehow for men to comprehend." Jesus felt his legs begin to tremble, as they sometimes did, and he held the soles of his feet squarely to the floor. The next sign was often a tic at the corner of his eye. He began to squint slightly to cover that spasm if it appeared. "There is a pattern for the Messiah that I must match, and men must feel threatened enough by my message to kill me to silence it. Otherwise I am no savior. I become only a man of the kind you prize so highly—living his own life, dying his own death."

The guard had risen from the table and walked to a barred window. He spoke with his back to Jesus. "A solution exists for you," he said, turning to look at his prisoner. "You may say that I am trying to trick you for reasons of my own, but that may not be the whole truth. Listen to me. Try to believe that I'm considering your interests as well as my own."

"You are going to suggest that I claim insanity."

"Why shouldn't you? We're doing several experiments with

mad prisoners. You would live at least another year or two. In that time you might be able to meet your requirement."

"If I began to help the insane—"

"If your presence jeopardized the work of our scientists, you would have to be killed."

"As a healer."

The guard's exasperation rose. "That's better, isn't it? You would be singled out. You would be put to death for a specific offense."

"It's better."

A clutching of skin at the corner of Jesus' eye was threatening to pull his face into a frown. He stroked the tight spot with his fingertip, hoping he was not drawing attention to his slow deliberate winking.

"I'll admit," the guard said, "that I would like to see you choose that course. You would be certified insane, and I could die free of you."

"They would not believe that I was mad."

"I have read the gospels carefully. Citing only their evidence, we can show that you are a lunatic—erratic in your moods, grandiose in your ambitions. The evidence is persuasive."

Jesus cracked at his knuckles but no sound came. "I might also be persuaded."

The guard bowed. "That would be more than I could ask."

"Because my message was so clear and the time so short," Jesus said, "I have been impatient. That much is true. I still believe that time is short, though the world has lasted many centuries past my expectation. Should the world go on forever, each man has only the same short life, and he needs every second for his salvation."

"You have been more than impatient. You have whipped and roared through the streets in a frenzy. The doctors will study that behavior all the more carefully since you were obsessed with love."

"They may invent some medical term for me."

"They needn't invent. The terms exist. For once you will be judged on earth by the standards applied to other men."

Jesus said, "I am not afraid."

The guard ignored him. "You needn't be afraid. You have said men are kind. That is true. They are much kinder than your God."

"I have been baited many times with those sentiments."

"You do accept the possibility that you are insane?" The guard had circled around his light remark, and he was doubling back in the hope Jesus had been serious.

"I told you that the possibility has troubled me. I have known the women who heard God urge them to kill their children. I've known kings and generals who claimed that God ordered their massacres. I've known too many of God's cronies and henchmen not to question how different I was."

"You've convinced yourself that you are different?"

"I speak for God. What those others may persuade themselves in no way compares with what I know. I pity them for their delusions, and I envy them for their freedom to invoke God for their own desires."

"I'm tempted to take you for a tour of our wards," the guard replied. "We have a cell filled with men who think they are Jesus Christ."

"Some may be right. God leaves nothing to chance, and as the number of men has grown, so has God increased his servants on earth. I would not be surprised to meet myself here, and when you began to speak so urgently to me, I wondered whether you were a Christ."

His words hit the guard with a force that caused him to slump far down in his chair. He looked afraid. "I have been gentle with you," he said softly. "The others wanted to beat you to get your true name. They wanted to thrust you in with the senile men and drooling women who think they are children again. Those old skeletons would crawl over your ankles,

pleading for candy, running at the nose and calling you 'Papa.'
The other guards wanted to test the fondness you profess
for children and see if your affection extended to old bones
starved back to happier days. I spared you that."

"Thank you."

"You owe me nothing. But I must tell you that I will not
tolerate more of your contempt. I have given you the reasons
I could not remain a Christian, and I will not permit you to
taunt me as a Christ."

"It was a first thought, nothing more. Men seldom care
about these questions unless they also have been marked for
my task. After you informed me so forcefully of your feelings,
I thought my error might amuse you."

"No," the guard said flatly, "I don't believe that. You know
exactly the kind of pain you can inflict, and you wanted to
see if you could hurt me. The answer is yes. That will not
save you."

"You made a choice," Jesus said, "and you claim to be content with it. You must see that your choice and mine are going to be different and that you look as mad to me as you say
I look to you."

"I am sane," the guard said without emphasis. "Sane
enough to reject your salvation."

Jesus answered, "I am sane enough to reject your escape."

"You are ready to die as a Jew?"

"There will be time again for me to die as a savior."

The guard caught him roughly by the arm. "Remember
that you are being killed for the accident of your race. In no
way is my country punishing you for your delusions."

"I will remember."

"At this moment I hate you enough to kill you myself."

With a tremor of hope, Jesus said, "Shoot me."

"No, I am going to cheat you as you have cheated every
man who swallowed your lies. Do you have a last word?"

"No."

"I am damned, of course?"

Jesus shook his head.

"Surely what I am doing guarantees my damnation?"

Jesus said, "You will be saved. You believe in me, and you will be saved."

"That is your idea of revenge?"

"I cannot tell you what you want to hear. You will be saved."

"I do not believe," the guard whispered.

"You will be saved."

The guard sprang at Jesus and struck him in the face with the butt of his pistol. He lashed three times across the bridge of the prisoner's nose. As Jesus sank toward the floor, the guard clubbed his skull. He stopped only to wipe the gun across his thigh and rub away the blood that made his fingers slip along the barrel. When he had finished, Jesus lay at his feet.

Lunging to the hall, the guard snapped his fingers to bring two young recruits running toward him. "Quickly!" he shouted when they came panting to his side. "An emergency!" He pointed to the body spread out on the concrete. "Get him out of here."

"To the hospital?" one boy asked.

"To chamber five, with the prisoners marked for two o'clock." The guard consulted his wristwatch. "You have only a minute. Hurry! He won't last until three."

"I don't understand," the boy said. The other recruit had taken Jesus by the shoulders and was trying to drag him out the door.

"It doesn't matter if you understand!" The guard had begun to weep. "Get him to the chamber before he dies." He beat on the recruit's arm until the two young men had raised Jesus and stumbled off with his body.

"Oh, God," the guard moaned as he watched their slow progress down the hall. "Don't let it be too late."

And when his friends heard of the crowds that pursued him, they went out to seize Jesus, for they said, "He is beside himself." By which they meant that he had not been so ecstatic when he lived among them in Galilee. By which they meant that his new fame grew from a sickness that made it shameful.

Jesus was retching behind a post when the chieftain caught up with him. "That one," Jesus said, pointing, "bring that boy to me."

The chief ran off and returned with a child of four or five. One of his legs was twisted until his toes spread backward. From his back, a hump grew like a woman's breast. Jesus did not look at the boy as he passed a hand rapidly over the swollen back and leg. With an exclamation of surprise, the boy found that he could straighten himself at both places. Saying nothing, he ran to hit a brother who was forever tormenting him.

"Thank you." As the boy had risen, the chief kneeled and used one of the few phrases he knew from the language Jesus spoke.

"I do it for myself," Jesus answered. "Their misery makes me sick. I know I must learn to bear it, as doctors do. But every time, I feel my stomach turning again, and I give in and heal them. Mine is the cowardly way, and yet how else could I preserve my compassion? I'd see the disease and senseless death, and my heart would harden until at last I could pass among the victims every day, setting bones, passing out pills and prescribing ointments. Since that's the modern way, I must learn it. What good is love that shrinks from open sores and lives on nothing but full and immediate cures? Without miracles, I will lose my ability to suffer, and yet the price of miracles is becoming too high." Jesus looked down ironically at the chieftain. "Of course you understand every word, and you're about to refute my misgivings with all your tribe's accumulated wisdom."

Bowing lower, the old man rubbed his cheek on Jesus' boot.

More than three hundred men and women had risen before dawn to attend the opening of the tomb. A large boulder covered the mouth of the cave, and John explained, shouting through his cupped hands, that the disciples sometimes had to unroll the rock themselves. Those women who had come as much to see an angel open the tomb as to see the risen Christ were disappointed. But they joined in the cheering as eight of the biggest volunteers put their shoulders to the rock.

Inside, the cave was dark. As the boulder fell away, the crowd surged forward to see what had been revealed. Their force pushed John headlong into the tomb, and he stumbled on the jagged ground where they had laid Jesus thirty-six hours before.

"Where is he?" the men at the back began to call. "Where is the risen Christ?"

"He is here," someone whispered near the entrance, and everyone was silent, and their silence troubled John more than the corpse at his feet. He knelt on the ground, shielding the body of Jesus from the sunlight entering the cave, and he prayed for a miracle that might confirm the multitude in its faith.

"Look!" cried a man at his elbow. "A flower!" He pulled from the ground a stalk with a gold stamen thrust out of waxy white petals. Those whose eyes could now see in the gloom of the cave shouted back to their neighbors outside, "A flower!

A flower has sprung up where the blood of Jesus had spilled."

The people, who asked far less from Christ than he had thought he must provide, went home to worship God and fix their Easter dinners.

(Unedited transcript. Read for revision and return to the committee offices.)

CHAIRMAN: We are continuing today with hearings on House Resolution 371, the bill that would prohibit all scientific experimentation on human reproduction and would provide penalties for interference, through pills, injections, machine rays or other means, with an unborn child's intelligence, physique or character.

BALTH: Out my way, Mr. Chairman, where a lot of good people are very much behind this bill, they're calling it the Unnatural Act. (*Laughter.*)

CHAIRMAN: It's that kind of approach we've been able to avoid thus far in these hearings. Our success may account for the limited public interest the first week of our investigation has occasioned. For my own part, I welcome the atmosphere of sober restraint that has allowed us to do our job quietly and efficiently.

MELCHIOR: Mr. Chairman, an executive from the Consolidated Broadcasting System has assured me that they will have a representative and full camera crew here tomorrow.

CHAIRMAN: Of course our doors will be open to them, as they have been open to any citizen interested in this vital legislation. I will now invite our first witness of the day to take his seat at the witness table and to state his name.

WITNESS: I am Jesus of Nazareth.

CHAIRMAN: I know from past hearings that I would only embarrass our distinguished guest if I began to recount his many honors and achievements. I would like to point out, however, that he has almost invariably placed high in the annual polls of most respected public figures, so his opinions today will undoubtedly reflect the sentiments of the many people who look to him for leadership.

MELCHIOR: But he is testifying only for himself.

CHAIRMAN: That is his practice, yes. I merely wanted to explain for the record why his request to appear was honored when many other applications had to be denied because of the limitations of time.

BALTH: I would be interested, Mr. Chairman, in seeing a list of the persons who were denied a chance to be heard.

CHAIRMAN: Such a list will be made available to the entire committee. Neither your chairman nor the staff has any wish to suppress dissent. Now let us proceed. Do you have a prepared statement, sir?

WITNESS: I have several preliminary remarks.

CHAIRMAN: Please proceed.

WITNESS: I have observed, from accounts of last week's hearings, that you have heard from scientists and lawyers, as well as from a sampling of this nation's clergymen. They have presented scientific, legal and ethical arguments for and against the proposed legislation. I am neither competent to join their debate nor interested in prolonging it on those levels. I asked to come here today to inform you of God's will.

MELCHIOR: Mr. Chairman, you assured us he was speaking only for himself.

BALTH: You know, Mr. Chairman, that the court has threatened to cite our whole committee for contempt if he starts talking about God again.

CHAIRMAN: I must ask the witness, while assuring him of my continued high esteem, to heed the objections of my colleagues. We are most interested in your viewpoint, sir, but there are certain limits we must ask that you respect.

WITNESS: May I continue?

CHAIRMAN: Please do.

WITNESS: I may state my message simply: God wants man to do whatever he can to improve the lot of his fellows.

MELCHIOR: Mr. Chairman!

CHAIRMAN: We will have to amend our transcript to offer that opinion as your own, sir. If you insist on bringing in concepts and phraseology prohibited to this committee, you will only succeed in making a lot of work for our stenographic staff.

BALTH: Mr. Chairman, he's been warned a hundred times. I don't mind saying that I was opposed to letting him come here again. You remember what happened during our hearing on sex offenders? A woman from his crowd bit the thumb off one of our policemen, Mr. Chairman.

WITNESS: Considering the nature of those hearings, it might have been worse. (*Laughter.*)

BALTH: I don't think contempt for the law is a laughing matter, Mr. Chairman. I, for one, would like to hear an apology from the witness for his blatant disregard of our rules before we proceed further.

CHAIRMAN: It is the view of the chair that our guest did not fully understand the nature of the restrictions imposed upon his appearance. If there is an apology to be made, I'll make it now to both the witness and the committee for not bringing more clarity to my exposition of our rules.

GASPAR: I would also like to apologize to the committee. I am sorry to have arrived late. But I would like to take this opportunity to say that our chairman is known to be one of the clearest men in our body.

MELCHIOR: One might even say one of the most transparent. (*Laughter.*)

CHAIRMAN: One might, but one would be out of order. (*Laughter.*) Now to continue: I think we can resolve this impasse if henceforth every time that the witness employs the prohibited terminology, our stenographer immediately substitutes the words "an influential friend of mine" or simply "my friend," as the context dictates. Is that acceptable?

BALTH: It'll keep us out of jail, anyway.

MELCHIOR: I would prefer use of the word "acquaintance" in place of "friend." I think the impressive testimony last week from our country's finest religious leaders of all faiths supports my substitution.

CHAIRMAN: They were pretty hard on you.

WITNESS: I've been hard on them.

CHAIRMAN: Rather than belabor the matter further, perhaps we could follow the lead of our friends in the television industry and substitute a "bleep" whenever the controversial word is used. Providing, of course, that the arrangement meets with the approval of the witness.

WITNESS: I've accepted cruder compromises than that.

CHAIRMAN: Thank you. Of course, in the transcript we will use a capital "B." Will you elaborate now, please,

on the brief statement you had made before this
lengthy digression.

WITNESS: As I understand their testimony, the clergymen
who spoke here claimed that to adjust malfunc-
tions in an embryo would be to usurp Bleep's
role.

CHAIRMAN: That is correct.

WITNESS: They don't realize that they are according him
powers he has never desired.

MELCHIOR: Surely the creation of life is not a human prerogative.

WITNESS: Not until man learns to do it.

GASPAR: May I say, speaking only for myself, that I will
be sorry to see the diversity pass out of human
life.

WITNESS: Which freaks and deviates will you miss? The
hunchbacks? The harelips? The imbeciles? The
insane? The woman with a blue birthmark running from her eyelid to her chin? The man with
testicles hanging to his knees?

GASPAR: Be that as it may, sir, a race of men as little dis-
tinctive as a drawer full of stainless steel dinner-
ware is not attractive to me.

WITNESS: Then you are ready to perpetuate human misery
for your own amusement? That is more than
Bleep would ask.

CHAIRMAN: He is willing to see men adjust and shape the
embryo to a standard mold?

WITNESS: He welcomes it. Were the job not so tedious, he
might have performed it himself.

BALTH: Some of us, who are a little bit skeptical of just
how authoritatively this witness can speak for any
outside power, believe that if men were all supposed to be the same, that's the way they'd have
been created. (*Applause.*)

WITNESS: Do members of this committee and this audience still use words like "created"? I thought I had been able at least to clear up that confusion. Man is an accident. While Bleep has assumed some responsibility, his capacity for attention and his interest in Earth are not great.

MELCHIOR: That's blasphemy, Mr. Chairman.

WITNESS: I would like to ask the representative a question, if I may?

MELCHIOR: I have no objection.

CHAIRMAN: Proceed.

WITNESS: Do you have children?

MELCHIOR: I do.

WITNESS: What are their ages?

MELCHIOR: I have a son twenty-eight years old and a daughter twenty-three.

WITNESS: Do they live at home?

MELCHIOR: No, they are both married. The boy is a chemist on the West Coast. The girl lives here in town.

WITNESS: Do you hear from them often?

MELCHIOR: Fairly often. Twice a week from our daughter. My son calls long-distance about once a month.

WITNESS: Always to ask for something?

MELCHIOR: Not at all. To find out how my wife and I are feeling and send his best wishes.

WITNESS: What would you think if every time he called he asked for money?

MELCHIOR: He wouldn't. That's not the way he was brought up.

WITNESS: You would see his dependence as not only unbecoming but as a reflection on you?

MELCHIOR: Certainly.

WITNESS: Your reaction would not be so very different from Bleep's. He is tired of hearing nothing from men but requests and appeals. If mankind starts to solve its own problems more efficiently, Bleep will consider that achievement the most satisfactory form of worship. There is also the other aspect that I mentioned—that he had not wanted man in the first place. To approximate Bleep's frame of mind, you'd have to imagine that you had not wanted your son—that he was conceived accidentally and has led to nothing but marriage and other irritations.

MELCHIOR: Mr. Chairman, I regard that as a slur on my wife and family.

WITNESS: I ask you to imagine such a situation, not confess to it.

CHAIRMAN: I think we'll move away from personalities, if you please.

GASPAR: I have a question for the witness. Surely Bleep demands that we believe in his existence?

WITNESS: Let me set a parallel for you. Picture yourself an extremely wealthy man.

GASPAR: A millionaire?

WITNESS: If that's the extent of your imagination. Now let me ask: Would you prefer that aborigines of the Out Back had never heard of you and doubted your existence? Or that they flooded your office with requests for money?

GASPAR: I—

WITNESS: I have known wealthy men, and they wanted above all to be left alone. Even the most generous of them hired someone else to dispose of their money. They found something unbecoming about sending off a donation to everyone who asked for one.

GASPAR: I can see that it would make them feel like cows, only good for milking.

WITNESS: Bleep long ago gave up trying to keep track of individual men. If a man has truly distinguished himself in some way, I have tried occasionally to bring him to Bleep's attention. But I have had trouble explaining why some of your artists are more esteemed than others. And he has never understood the loathing inspired by the losing generals in your wars. Often, before one of these interviews, Bleep asks absently whether man is the animal with the antlers or the elongated neck. I grant that he does it to bait me, but you can see that questions of that sort disrupt any serious discussion.

GASPAR: But he must want to know that men believe in him.

WITNESS: How would you react if I told you I did not believe that you existed? (*Laughter.*)

GASPAR: I'd think you were crazy. (Laughter; applause.)

WITNESS: Would you curse me or try to scourge me?

GASPAR: I'd feel sorry for you.

WITNESS: Yes.

CHAIRMAN: We are straying from the topic. The witness was assuring us that no repercussions would be felt if man began to assume responsibilities that hitherto have not been his.

WITNESS: None at all. I think we would all hope that man would improve on Bleep's handiwork. That should not be hard. I have often taxed Bleep with some oddity in man's physique or psychology, only to have him shrug and say, "I'm not a doctor or a sculptor. Your men are lucky to be alive at all. Let them work out their own details."

CHAIRMAN: Has he ever given hints as to improvements he would welcome?

WITNESS: I don't think it's possible to exaggerate his indif-
ference. Oh, on one occasion I heard him com-
ment on man's unimaginative use of time.

CHAIRMAN: Could you explain?

WITNESS: He seems to find man's insistence on the present
a little stifling, a little dull. He's complained once
or twice that men could live more sensibly if they
would give up their dependence on sequential
time.

CHAIRMAN: Live in the past and future at once?

WITNESS: Alternate. I know for a fact that he thinks a fore-
taste of age and pain would heighten the pleasures of youth. I've told him he's wrong. He
doesn't appreciate the human mania for ignorance.

CHAIRMAN: None of our scientists' experiments so far have
permitted us to hope for such mastery of time.

WITNESS: You asked what he had spoken about. I took one
of the few examples I could remember.

CHAIRMAN: However, we can now change skin color, hair
color, eye color, sex, height, weight and the intelligence level of the unborn. Would there be objection to that?

WITNESS: What color is a housefly?

CHAIRMAN: Transparent on the wings, I think—green and
black on the body. A little red, and some irides-
cent patches, as I recall.

WITNESS: What if I told you that there are fifty-four different colors and combinations of houseflies?

CHAIRMAN: I'd be interested.

WITNESS: Overwhelmingly interested?

CHAIRMAN: Mildly interested.

WITNESS: What if I told you that the flies were able to
control those combinations and would begin
shortly to produce flies that were more attractive

to other flies or better adapted to their environment? Would you feel betrayed or cheated by those changes?

BALTH: Mr. Chairman, is the witness implying that Bleep's interest in mankind is the same as man's interest in the common housefly?

WITNESS: Much less.

BALTH: I would like to say for the record that the credibility of the witness has been very much undercut by the tenor of his remarks today.

GASPAR: I do think the witness should know that the sponsors of the bill, testifying last week, left us with the impression that Bleep's wrath would be great indeed if we permitted the kind of adjustment and control our scientists have made available to us.

WITNESS: What form would this wrath take?

GASPAR: They didn't specify.

WITNESS: Famine? Floods? Fire? Plagues?

CHAIRMAN: This is not exactly in your domain, but I worry about another aspect: Which of us is intelligent and decent enough to supervise these experiments?

WITNESS: If such a superior man existed, your scientists would not have had to work so long to allow you to create him. They have given you tools. Now you can breed the kind of men you wish you were.

CHAIRMAN: There are a dozen more questions we could explore today, but our time is running short. I would like to ask the indulgence of the committee to raise a final point with the witness, one that I take up with apprehension. What will be the result of our experiments, if they are successful, on your work?

WITNESS: On my mission?

CHAIRMAN: I can foresee a time when men will come to be-
              lieve your stories of Bleep's indifference. When
              they reach that point, will you be able to bridge
              so enormous a gap for them?

WITNESS: I am urging men to improve themselves so they
              might interest Bleep without my intervention.

CHAIRMAN: Is that possible?

WITNESS: When man has learned to control his world,
              when he can ring up the dawn and bring out the
              stars, when he can inject life instead of only ex-
              tracting it, when he has found the way to harness
              time and make it do his bidding, when he has
              learned to control his world and himself, then
              Bleep may not find man's presence insufferable.

CHAIRMAN: But what need would such men have for Bleep?

MELCHIOR: Before you get started on all of that, I'd like to
              point out that it's lunchtime, Mr. Chairman.

BALTH: I would remind my esteemed colleagues that
              these hearings have not been concluded. Tomor-
              row we will be privileged to hear from one of my
              most distinguished constituents, an internation-
              ally esteemed man of Bleep, who assures me he
              can refute everything said here today.

MELCHIOR: I, for one, look forward to hearing a more bal-
              anced presentation.

CHAIRMAN: As I have said so often, this committee wants to
              hear all sides of an issue before we pass on the
              legislation.

WITNESS: There is only one side, and I have presented it.

MELCHIOR: May I move, Mr. Chairman, that today's hearing
              be adjourned?

BALTH: I second the motion.

CHAIRMAN: The hearings stand adjourned. I would like to
              invite the witness to join the committee members
              and staff in our cafeteria for luncheon.

WITNESS: Thank you, but I'm due across the corridor in
             ten minutes for a hearing on compound interest
             rates.

From the edge of the crowd, Jesus saw a boy about sixteen
being pushed into the square. His eyes had rolled upward
with fright until their whites pleaded blankly for his life.
"What was his crime?" Jesus asked a priest.

"He cut the head off a crucifix." The man was sour with
sweat. Turning from Jesus he shouted, "Death! Death now!"

The rest happened rapidly, and only the cries of the crowd,
which saw with one quick eye, told Jesus that the punishment
had been performed. At the end, he could make out a head
being pulled up from the boy's neck, pulled higher until the
body fell backward and the bloody head swung free in a soldier's fist. "Hurrah!" the crowd's voice cried. "Death to the
Christ-killer!"

The body was thrown into a fire, where it roasted slowly.
In the boy's coat pocket the soldiers had discovered a book
by the cleverest man of the age. Its pages burned more
brightly than the corpse.

"He read too much," the priest said to Jesus, when the
crowd's eye closed and each man regained his sight.

"Was that a Bible in his pocket?" Jesus knew it was not.

"Of course not." The priest's indignation had been spent
and he answered listlessly. "Who has ever been corrupted by
the Bible?"

They sat across from each other at a small table, separated
only by noise and smoke. "Do you come here often?" Pilate
asked.

They had been drinking for more than three hours, and Jesus' voice was strained. "Oh, once in a while."

"It's a very stimulating atmosphere," Pilate said for the second time.

The music had begun again, all brass and electronic strings. Jesus said, "What?"

"I'm glad we came here."

"Good place." Jesus nodded with finality. "I come here all the time."

"Expensive, though."

"What?"

"I said, it's not cheap."

Jesus looked hurt and confused. "It's not cheap."

"That's what I said."

"The noise." Jesus felt his head spin and a fissure open at the back of his skull. He rarely drank. "You know," he said, "I'm a good man."

"Yes," Pilate answered, not quite a question.

"Nothing has touched my spirit. It's pure. Even with all this, even after so many times, I haven't changed. I can't change."

"That's good."

"It's not good." Jesus pushed his empty glass to the edge of the table. "It's not bad. It's the way it is, not good, not bad."

A waiter brought them each another drink. Had he looked first to Pilate with a cocked eyebrow? Had Pilate nodded before Jesus could be served? Jesus could not be sure. He thought he had seen a glance exchanged. "I have within me," Jesus said, "unsullied purity that speaks to every man. By accepting all wounds I have kept myself unscathed. By assuming all burdens I have never been fettered."

"Is that so?"

"Are you telling me to be quiet?"

"Not at all." Pilate was confident enough to withstand inquiring or amused looks from the other tables. But since he was not interested in drunken boasts, he tried to look self-conscious. "The music has stopped. We don't want to disturb these other people."

"Sure! Sure we do! We want to wake them up. Right now! We want them to hear about me. About my purity. We want them to envy me and see that they can never be as pure as I am."

"Why?"

"They've got to be unhappy." Jesus banged his glass. "They've got to be miserable that they can't be me."

"What good is that?"

"It helps." Jesus screwed up his face cannily. "It helps."

"Wouldn't they be helped more by being left alone?"

Jesus rolled the bottom of his pure silk tie with surprisingly steady fingers. "I mean, it helps me."

In unison now, who is the son of God?
You are.
Once again and louder.
YOU ARE!
And how do you know?
YOU TOLD US SO!
Class dismissed.

Some Saturday afternoons Pilate came to see him at the headquarters. Until they had moved in precinct maps and campaign literature, the building had been a supermarket with a large rear entrance and an acre of parking space. Pilate left his car there and came in the back way. Jesus worked in the cubicle nearest the alley entrance and no one saw Pilate enter or leave. It was an arrangement that suited both of them.

Jesus had been interviewing applicants all day, and he looked up gratefully when Pilate entered. He could justify their friendship more easily than Pilate could. But he knew that his official reasons, all impeccable, were not the true ones.

"I passed one of your workers as I came in," Pilate said as greeting. "Can't they learn to breathe through their noses?"

"His mouth was open?"

"Any slacker and he'd need a hinge. Where do you find them?"

"One man tells another. We get more applicants than we can use. I'd thought of advertising, but it's expensive and we're short of money. Unless you'd like to volunteer space in your papers?"

"Only on the comic page."

"We had ten applicants today for one job. You saw the last one."

"It's your fault for insisting on workingmen. I say you should get more professional people."

"The last fellow you recommended called himself an administrative assistant."

Pilate managed to look urbanely discomfited. "He'd have done you more good than the abalone fisherman you finally took. You're too nostalgic."

"Probably."

"What do you look for when you interview them? Besides infinite credulity?"

Jesus leaned back in his chair and closed his eyes. "What do I look for or what do I get?"

"Both."

"I look for intelligent, resourceful, decent, sensitive young men with agreeable manners and the ability to amuse me."

"What do you get?"

"Believers. Because they're the ones who can do the job. The others would be more pleasant around here, but we'd end up with a social club. So I get neurotic, angry, resentful, impatient, abrasive crackpots and cranks. That's why we have to talk so much about love. I can soften a tough man more easily than I can toughen a soft one."

Pilate picked at the crease in his pin-striped trousers. "Why can't they be a little brighter?"

"Intelligence would be a handicap. You've pointed that out often enough. If I haven't agreed with you before, it's because I hadn't gone through a day like this one."

"You're finally admitting that your enterprise is built on sham?"

Jesus began weeding his mail, tossing most letters into the green wastebasket beside his desk. "No, it hasn't been that bad. But I've never ranked intelligence at the top of human virtues. You only need intelligence when you don't have faith, and even then it's not enough. I get exasperated with my men, but they're the best I can find. You, for example, wouldn't do."

"I'm not looking for work."

"Good."

"All of your men aren't the same, though. You must have different requirements for different jobs. Simon Peter is not Philip, after all."

"That's right. I look for complementary traits, strengths to balance weaknesses. By now I have a pretty fair idea of what we need."

"What do you look for in Peter?"

Careful. Today I need to talk, but I cannot be frank with Pilate. He will find a way to betray me, and that job is already taken. "Peter?"

"Yes."

The true administrative assistant, though he would have sense enough to shun the title. A man loyal to me as the head of a business but eager in his heart to step in and take charge. Enough polish to be able to work with other men and win over the skeptical. I pick an older man each time. For the reassurance my earthly family did not give me? That would be the popular opinion and so, probably wrong. Because I exert my authority more fully in front of the others by giving orders to a man twenty years my senior? Or simply because the kind of competence I need is acquired only through age? "Peter must be sensible and loyal," Jesus said. "I once called him my rock."

"Because he was strong or because you wanted him to be strong?"

If you knew Peter, you would not have to ask. "Your questions show the gulf that separates us. I'll never learn to think so subtly."

"If you didn't purport to be the Son of God, I'd make a rude remark."

"Ask about Andrew. He's easier to explain."

"What about him?"

Good sense dictates that one of the men be a brute, and the fact that he is Simon's brother gives me a measure of control over him. When the local residents have seen too much of John or Thaddaeus, I parade Andrew past them to ease their minds. "He's forthright and practical, the kind of man you'd put in charge of each of your departments if you could get enough of them. I'm lucky to find one."

"You inherit him through his brother. He'd never come to you on his own."

You're right. "You're wrong."

"Philip?"

Slick. "Informed."

"Matthew?"

Stupid. "Cautious."

"John?"

Ah, John. My mother loves herself through me. The other men love the God I can sometimes reveal to them. But John loves me, and if I don't return his love, it may be that I find it too important to give up. "John has the insights of a tender nature."

"He does you no good."

"No?"

"People don't like him. They find him queer."

Queer. A good, shriveled word. I find John queer too, but the word is not a curse to me. I use his queerness, as I use Peter's gift for leadership or Matthew's penchant for taking notes on every trivial conversation. I see a longing in John's eyes that has nothing to do with mansions in heaven. I pretend to miss his meaning, and I talk with greater force about salvation, and I watch his longing grow until it passes out of passion and we are talking about the same thing after all. If John asked me to cure him, I could. But he would get to heaven no faster, and we might both regret the queerless path he had chosen. "I've never seen anything like that."

"I don't mean he's guilty of any offense. It's his manner."

"He's dedicated."

Pilate seemed to regret his criticism. "I'm sure he's fine in his own way. He makes me feel uncomfortable, that's all."

"That's part of our job. We're supposed to make you uncomfortable. Don't I?"

"No, you don't." As he stood, Pilate drummed his fingers on the edge of Jesus' desk. "Quite the contrary. I leave here feeling very good." He was a man keen for every truth but happy ones. With effort he said, "I'm glad you let me come."

"I keep expecting to pick up a paper one day and find that you've endorsed me."

"You know there's no chance of that."

Jesus took the hand Pilate extended. "I deal in hope," he said. "I have supplies you can't exhaust."

"Good-bye," Pilate said. "Forget what I told you about John."

"What could you tell me about John?"

When, equally perfect, he was passed over yet again, Jesus murmured, "*Lama sabachtani.*" After so long a time, he found the Aramaic words came readily to his tongue.

"And?"

"The conjunction," Jesus explained to Mark. "It's a word that's taken each of the unconnected events in my life and joined them and given them direction. At those times that I've lost sight of my goal, I have had to be grateful for 'and.'"

"And that's why when I asked you what you thought was the most beautiful word in the language, you said—"

"And."

"Doesn't it seem odd," Pilate asked, "that none of your disciples came from the ranks of men you healed? Of those you cured of blindness, lameness, of those you brought to life again, none of them chose to join you. Doesn't that seem odd?"

"It seems odd that it seems odd to you," Jesus replied. "You're renowned for your cynicism."

Pilate thought for a moment and said, "I understand."

"None of the men I cured betrayed me. If you're looking for an oddity, explain that."

"I don't understand everything," Pilate said. He sat as though musing, to delay the moment that he had to summon the elders and deliver his verdict. "I'm not cynical enough to understand everything."

"Heal me!" the old cripple called.

"Why?"

"Because I cannot walk. I cannot work. I must beg money from the strangers on the street."

"Did you like to work?"

"I hated it."

"But you hate begging more?"

"I can go on begging after you heal me. No one has to know that I can walk."

"Then why do you ask to be healed?"

"For the afterlife," the cripple said. "I don't want to be maimed for eternity."

You support me in my lies, Jesus thought. I will not complain about yours. He said, "Get up."

The cripple looked down the street. "Is anyone watching?"

"No," said Jesus, "no one."

Mail was delivered to his block very late in the day. Jesus blamed the large number of widows who lived on all sides of him in small houses and shabby apartment buildings. The sight of the mailman was the day's highlight for them, and they lay in wait in their hallways to trap him for a few words when he arrived with bills and advertising circulars.

Jesus expected no mail, but he found himself sitting on the porch and waiting as impatiently as the widows for the mailman's appearance. It was his second of three chances to hear God. He had already paced along the sea before dawn to listen to the roll of the waves. Then he hurried back to his doorstep to overhear scraps of talk from the women who had

snared the postman. He vaguely recalled that once his instructions had come coded in one of their chance remarks,
and he had no better plan than to wait again and listen. The
third chance came each night after his street was quiet and
he could walk along the pavement, looking down at the cracks
or up at the sky.

I do not mind this watching and waiting now, he said to
God. But I would not like to wear these frayed and gritty
trousers when I am forty. Then I don't want to walk this
street every day still trying to learn your plan for me. I want
to be dead by forty with my job done.

At forty he repeated the same words, setting sixty as his
limit.

When they did bury him many years later, he was wearing
trousers that were frayed but clean. The widows, who had
hoped toward the end that he might marry one of them, remarked fondly on how faithful he had been about taking his
exercise.

Jesus was sitting by the window of his room when, without
knocking, Thomas burst upon him. "It's not true, is it, Lord?"

An ache in his legs had kept Jesus awake all night. Before
midnight he had begun taking the medicine that helped him
ignore pain, and the bottle was nearly empty. He looked
through the window to the point where he had seen Thomas
on the road a minute ago. Could Thomas be here? Was this
the Thomas he had seen outside only two beats of his pulse
ago? Or were there Thomases to walk in the road and
Thomases to rush through doors and Thomases to shout distraught questions?

"We are all so worried, Lord," this Thomas said, moving
closer, speaking more deliberately. "They want me to learn
from you that it is not true."

"What?" Jesus asked. He was distantly aware that he had asked a question. He thought he might have asked the Thomas that stood before him which Thomas he was.

"That you have sold your soul to the Devil." Thomas was a young man, round at the hips, a purveyor of gossip; for all of that, an upright man in what he did for his wife and children. "We have heard that since God no longer speaks to you, you have turned against him and will try to lead us into evil."

Jesus had not heard the question, but he answered, "No." Something told him that Thomas was expecting the answer, Yes. Instead, he said, "No," and braced himself to meet Thomas' protest. He could feel a wave of disappointment pouring from the young disciple, who had dropped to his knees and was kissing Jesus' fingers.

"Forgive me," Thomas said. "I should not even have asked." Jesus missed the words but heard the disappointment. He pulled his mind in focus that he might end their interview coherently.

"I hope," Jesus said, trying to sound kindly, "that the others won't be as sorry as you are."

He watched Thomas backing through the door, Thomas watching him with horror, or contempt, or was it nothing but fresh disappointment? The picture troubled Jesus for a moment until he saw the real Thomas appear safely again on the road below the window. The shape of this Thomas swelled up at the head and shrank at the shoulders as Jesus watched him through the bottom of his bottle.

A headline read, "Mortuary Finds 'Dead' Woman Alive." Jesus quickly turned the page. He read the newspaper less attentively than usual, folded it back into shape and carried it to the incinerator. He had a match lit before he relented and reached into yesterday's ashes for the page with the story about an old woman returning to life.

Doctors from the city's health department explained that no heartbeat had been heard when the woman had been pronounced dead. "A person can pass into a state of deep syncope, and the appearance and condition of the patient can simulate death very closely," one doctor was quoted as saying.

Jesus replaced the paper in the burner and struck another match. Now they call it syncope. One name is as good as another. Let them use any scientific word they like. Let them try to explain away with new words what they can never understand. When they take refuge in syncopes and simulation, they admit that I did more than they can dream of doing. Nothing any man can do could jeopardize me. I am not man and not confined by his successes. Let them bring a thousand old women back to life with needles and shocks. That is nothing compared to one resurrection through faith. They will find that faith begins where their science has ended.

The wind was high, and Jesus lit a dozen matches before he got the paper burning.

Jesus had begun to dream every night. He resented dreaming, and he refused the next morning to remember messages that had come to him, not from God but from a part of himself that had nothing to tell him.

I will not beg. Whatever you ask, I will do. But you must ask. Too many men have wept away their lives praying for a small sign from you. When your will was carved into my flesh, I despised their tears and their despair. I knew that I might fail you but that you could not fail me. The worst of my lives promised me nothing less than perfect faith.

For what you then gave freely, I will not beg you now. Neither your commandments nor the nature of the world has changed. You need me no more nor less than the first time or the last.

To shame the proud men, I have been meek. To you alone, I have revealed the fullness of my pride. I have used your name on Earth. I have invoked your power until men mistook me for the God I came to glorify. Their praise filled my ears but it never touched my heart. I learned to turn their worship back to you, and I moved forward without tripping on the bodies at my feet. My humility was perfect and, if your trust in me had continued, I could have kept my head bowed through eternity.

But remember: You taught me to assume God's bearing. Remember: You forced me to speak with God's voice. If you withdraw your grace from me, I have light to lift your shadow from the earth. It is my light, God. I will not beg for another chance to be your dim reflection.

"Have you heard today?"

"Nathanael, I will tell you when I have heard."

"How long has it been since God spoke to you?"

"I don't keep count. A long time."

"We are all praying."

"For me?"

"For you, and for ourselves."

"Cheer up."

"I feel so bad. I would do anything I could to make God speak."

"No one makes God speak. He does not respond to threats."

"Have you tried?"

"What? Warnings that I would shame him, repudiate him, ignore him?"

"He must learn that you will not wait forever."

"Unless he knows already that I will."

"We are all to wait? To go on with our prayers unanswered through another dozen lifetimes? We cannot."

"You sound mutinous, Nathanael, you who are so patient in everything else."

"Nothing else matters."

"Other things must begin to matter for you."

"James says you told him to get a hobby."

"He has a sharp tongue. I was not so fatuous."

"After God, any interest is a hobby."

"I am not saying that you must forget God."

"You aren't? You're not saying that?"

"Not yet."

Joseph had died when Jesus was nineteen. Telling his story to an alienist, Jesus mentioned the simple burial his family had arranged.

The doctor's interest, which had been simmering, flared. "You were nine, you say?"

"Nineteen."

The doctor allowed the corners of his eyelids to droop. "For a minute, I thought we had something."

Once: "He's only drunk," Jesus told the widow of Lazarus angrily. "You can tell—look at all these bottles. It's too much wine."

"Oh!" she moaned, her head covered with the black scarf

she wore on Sundays. "Oh! He's dead! He's dead! You can bring him back to life. Doctor, save him!"

Jesus had been dragged by the arm down the dirt road. He was heavy in the belly and not used to running. At the sick man's bedside he was puffing.

From his bag he brought out a vial with an odor so sharp that his own nostrils burned when he pulled its cork. He shoved the tube under Lazarus' nose and kept one hand on his pulse. The drunken man stirred to pull his face away from the spirits. Deep in his throat he coughed a protest.

"You see, he lives. Your husband will recover."

She knelt before him, but he pulled her roughly to her feet. "None of that."

"Oh, Doctor, tell me how I can repay you? What can I give you for this miracle?"

"I had no patients. There will be no fee. But do not use that word again."

"Why—?"

"There are no miracles—only knowledge and hard work."

"Doctor," the woman said, "I was wrong. You are the amazement. You are the true son of—" She paused for prompting.

"Science."

"The true son of science," she repeated reverently.

When Paul held open his arms, Jesus moved forward with the rest of the audience. Monitors were watching every row, and Jesus thought he would be less noticeable moving with the crowd. He drifted with the other men and women down the concrete steps and across the green turf of the playing field. He had been sitting far back in the stadium. By the time he reached the platform, the pledging ceremony was nearly over.

From his height, Paul looked down sharply at him, glanced away, looked back and stared at the top of Jesus' bowed head. He murmured something to an attendant and soon the man was at Jesus' side.

"Paul of Tarsus would like to see you," the man said, "when the others leave."

"I can't stay."

The man was fleshy, but he looked desperate enough to be dangerous. "You must talk with him. He's been waiting for you in every city."

"All right."

"He'll go to that trailer behind the platform for his dinner."

"I'll join him."

"Thank you," the man said before he hurried back to Paul's side. "Thank you."

Jesus walked as slowly as he could to the trailer's door. The way was blocked by a tall man with a beaked nose. "No admittance," he said.

"All right."

Jesus turned away, but Paul had reached them, and he pulled Jesus into the trailer.

The beak-nosed man and another, bigger man began to lift Paul out of his dark blue suit. Jesus could see that sweat had turned its white lining yellow. He had read once that Paul wore his suits three times, then threw them out. The men pulled off Paul's underwear and rubbed him with a long white towel. When Paul was dry, the second man brought out a monogrammed red silk robe and draped it around Paul's big sturdy body.

"You came," Paul said when the men had left.

"Yes."

"Did you see the empty chair on the platform? I told you that was for you."

"I liked sitting at the back. I could see better. Up there the lights are so strong."

"They are very strong." Peter rubbed at his blond curls with the long towel. "That's the reason for those suits. Anything cheaper rots away."

"Yes."

"You don't believe me. You think I like luxury too much."

"You work very hard."

"That's right." Was Paul becoming angry? Jesus thought he was; he always did. "I work hard every day, every week. I've worked for years. For you."

"I know."

"Did you watch them tonight? Did you see them change? It's that way every time. They come as forty thousand lost beings, and I meld them and join them into one throat that sings your praise. Did you see that?"

"You have a gift."

"That's right," Paul said again. "I have a gift."

The men brought in a large beefsteak, a flagon of red wine and two plates and glasses. Jesus pushed his away, and Paul began to drink. He had finished half the steak when the man who had asked Jesus to come appeared at the door with a small card which he set before Paul.

Paul read the amount aloud to Jesus. "That's the largest sum ever collected in this country," Paul said. "Only three times have we gotten more, and never from a crowd that size. They were moved, if you weren't."

"I wanted to see you."

"To go back and tell the others how gross I've become? Is that why you came? To shame me? To leave me filled with doubt?"

Flee, Jesus' heart told him. Flee before you bury his small doubts under your own.

Paul held his tears in the corners of his eyes. "What do I do wrong?"

"Nothing," Jesus said mildly. "I don't want to disappoint you."

"You already disappoint me." Heat from his rising anger had dried his tears. "You are the disappointment of my life. I've told a thousand stories about you—about fire banked in ashes, glory hidden in human form. And now you give me—"

"Only the ashes, only the poor body."

"I don't mind that." Wine had left stains on the polished surfaces of his teeth. "I have fire enough for both of us. I can restore your visions and make you live for others as you will no longer live for yourself."

"I can't help you. I came to tell you."

"Then don't hurt me."

"I don't want to hurt you."

"When I look into your eyes, let me see more than myself."

Jesus kept his eyes on Paul.

"If I thought you had fallen beneath me," Paul said, "my heart would break but I could go on."

"Think that."

"I see you rising above me and you won't show me the way to your side. I can only follow the God you were. You won't let me near the man you've become."

"Follow God."

Paul's handsome face was heavy. "I want to follow you."

Jesus walked out of the trailer and onto the playing field, where the grass was already moist beneath his feet.

Royalties from his book had permitted Matthew to buy a suit of Scotch tweed and English tailoring. Peter braced himself for a scene when Jesus first encountered Matthew and his new suit on the street. Instead, Jesus complimented its close weave and fine workmanship. As they walked on, Jesus remarked that since Matthew's position demanded a good appearance, he might as well buy durable clothes. And Peter reflected that he had won another of those arguments he preferred to lose.

"Doubt is the leavening that makes faith rise," one disciple said.

Then they all joined in:

"Doubt is the alloy that makes faith endure."

"Doubt is the shadow faith casts at men's feet."

"Doubt is the blemish that makes faith's beauty endurable."

Jesus composed his own versions and posted them on the bulletin board in the hall:

Doubt is the coffee break in faith's routine.

Doubt is the black root of an angel's blond faith.

Doubt is the knot in faith's muscle and the cramp from faith's plenty.

Doubt is the runt in faith's litter.

Doubt is the one reward faith can ever offer.

The disciples read his note with dismay.

Jesus gave no thought to the Devil. He had found that when God withdrew, all temptation ended. He did not consider this discovery anything more than he had known throughout his life. All the same, he was surprised.

His mother met him in the hospital corridor, outside an open door. "She's been asleep all morning," Mary whispered, "but she seems to be coming around now."

"What does the doctor say?"

"That she won't last through the night."

"Have you tried to speak with her?"

"Last night I asked some questions and told her to blink if she wanted to answer yes. She recognized me—at least she seemed to—and when I asked her if I should call you, she blinked four or five times."

"Let's go in."

She held back. "First, what are you going to tell her?"

"Nothing. I want to see her before she dies."

"She has believed you."

"I know," Jesus said.

"You can't go in and hurt her."

"Let me go."

Mary took away her hand. "Don't hurt her."

Jesus passed one empty bed in the room and approached the second, where Mary Magdalene lay by the window. She was coated with plaster and rolled in blankets, and her head had been shaved before the doctors decided that an operation would not help. Clear plastic tubes ran from inside each nostril to a receptacle hidden among the pillows behind her head. The tubes swept up the front of her face and over the shaved surface of her skull. As she exhaled, a milky fluid from her nose appeared for an instant in the tubes. It was sucked out of sight when she breathed in.

"Maggie," Jesus' mother whispered. "Are you awake?"

The eyes in the face were open.

"Remember what we did last night? If you hear me, blink your eyes." The lashes dropped once and rose again. "She doesn't hear you," Jesus said. "That's a reflex."

"Yes, she hears me. Don't you, dear?" The eyes stayed open. "We won't tire you with a lot of questions. You lie there and relax. Do you see who's come to visit you?"

Intending to smile, Jesus found himself frowning into her eyes. "Hello."

The white fluid spurted up in the tube. Slowly it drained back in her nostrils.

"Do you recognize Jesus?" his mother asked. "Blink once if you recognize him."

"Never mind," Jesus said. His voice had made the white fluid shoot up again, and he took Mary Magdalene's cold hand reassuringly. "How can we go for walks if you don't get better?" he asked the open eyes. "You know I don't get enough exercise unless you come and pull me outside."

"Oh, Maggie doesn't want to think about walks right now," Mary crooned. "She knows she's not going to get well. She's not afraid to die either. That's right, isn't it, dear?"

The eyes closed and did not open. In the tubes liquid rose and fell steadily with no sign that Mary's question had disturbed the girl. "Maggie, Jesus came to tell you about dying," his mother said. "He came here to help."

Jesus let her speak.

Mary said, "Maggie, if you're hearing me, dear, just blink your eyelids again, one time." The lids jumped. "Good. That's fine, dear. Now pay attention to Jesus. Listen to what he's going to tell you. It'll make everything much easier for you. Listen to him."

Jesus' silence forced her to go on.

"He's going to tell you about heaven, and about God's love. You know that God is waiting to welcome you into his arms, and that's why you had the accident. God wants you with him."

Fluid spurted up the tubes, almost to the line where her dark hair had been shaved. "You're upsetting her," Jesus said.

"No, this is a comfort. If this is comforting, if our visit is helping you, blink your eyes, dear." The lids opened slowly. Jesus saw nothing in the eyes.

"I know you have many questions, Maggie," his mother said soothingly. "But we'll take them one at a time. Jesus will answer for you. You lie back, and I'll ask everything you'd want to ask yourself. First, are you going to heaven? That's right, isn't it? Don't try to blink. It's natural that you'd want to know. Jesus will tell you. Maggie's going to heaven, isn't she, son?"

"She's not hearing any of this. We should go."

Mary's face was composed and gentle. "No, we're going to stay and answer her questions. Maggie's not going to die without the answers she deserves. We're going to do that for her."

He saw that he could not bring himself to leave alone. "All right."

"Maggie, listen to Jesus. Is our friend here going to heaven soon? Will all her suffering be ended? Will she dwell forever in the house of the Lord?"

"Yes," Jesus said.

The eyes in the face did not move, and the fluid in the tubes registered nothing.

Mary spoke again, swaying to the cadence of her own soft voice. "Will we all be united once more in the mansions of heaven? Will we find together the peace that has escaped us on earth? Will we be ushered into the presence of God our father?"

"Yes."

"And all our doubts will be forgotten, and all our despair will be forgotten, and death will never be able to touch us again?"

Jesus looked to the bed where the eyes were open but the chest was still. "She's dead."

"Will the beauty of God's love fill our souls?" Mary reached forward to lower the girl's eyelids. "Will the joy of knowing God make all the misery of our lives look insignificant? Will God's glory at last make each of us glorious?"

She was still talking when Jesus went out the door.

James came to say, "Don't feel that you've let us down, Lord. Don't think that you've failed us."

"You?" Jesus was too puzzled to watch his words. "What does it have to do with you?"

Jesus overheard the apostles speaking again of the mystery of life. The phrase annoyed him, and he demanded that they produce a list of the elements that made up that mystery. Andrew came dutifully to him the next day with a single typewritten page.

What is life?
Why do men live?
What is love?
Is love good for men or bad?
Why is incest attractive?
Why is incest forbidden?
Have we lived before?
Will we live again?
Why does every man hope to fail, suffer and die?
Why does every man fight to dominate, inflict pain and live?

Jesus counted. "Ten?" he asked. "Can your fabled mystery be reduced to ten simple questions?"

"Simon wanted to know why certain sounds and certain sights please us and others sicken us," Andrew said. "We thought that was one of the secondary questions that we didn't need to trouble you with. John wanted to know why he grits his teeth when he strokes his favorite cat. Those were the only things we eliminated."

"Who is obsessed with incest?" Jesus asked.

"Your brother, Lord. He thinks many other questions would be unnecessary if those two were answered honestly."

"There's nothing personal in his interest?"

Andrew kept his eyes on the list and refused to smile.

"You'd have to ask him, Lord. We agreed to put in his questions because nobody wanted to have to argue against them."

Jesus folded the paper twice and slipped it into the top
drawer of his desk. "From now on, when we talk about life,
let us address ourselves to one of these questions. Don't you
agree, Andrew? We needn't waste any more time with beautiful evasions like 'mystery.' "

"Yes, Lord."

Jesus was about to return to his work when an oversight
on the list struck him. He drew out the paper and read it
through again. "You don't ask if there is a God." He was delighted to see Andrew begin to blush.

"We thought it wasn't a good time to raise all that," he
said wretchedly. "We thought if you knew, you would have
told us before this."

"You do me no favor, Andrew," Jesus said, "holding back
the one true question. Here—" he threw the list over the
desk top—"I am proving that men want to be hurt. Hurt
me."

At the top of the page, Andrew wrote in a haphazard scrib-
ble that made the typewritten words look false and faraway,
"Is there a God?" He pushed the list back to Jesus.

"The answer to your last question—which has become your
first question—is no," Jesus said. "You'll forgive me if I don't
want to plunge immediately into something so timely and
vital as why a boy shouldn't ravage his mother?"

"Of course, Lord." The pain Jesus was causing Andrew
showed in his face.

"We'll take up the rest of them again," Jesus said, replacing
the list in his drawer. "I may even produce a different answer
to the question we have already settled."

"When one answer doesn't satisfy a man, Lord," Andrew
said timidly, "he searches for another. That's science."

"That's hypocrisy." Jesus turned away so Andrew would
leave. "But I've not shut hypocrisy out of my life, and we

may as well not trouble our friends with the answer to a question they didn't ask."

"You can trust me, Lord."

The look Jesus gave him sent Andrew hurrying from the room.

Jesus!

Who is it?

It's God, Jesus. Listen to me.

It's not God. It's one of my own voices.

Believe me.

It's a voice I've heard coming from my own heart.

Please.

You've fooled me too often.

Trust me.

I will trust you as my own voice. You have as much right to speak as any of my other voices.

Trust me as God.

No.

This is your last chance.

You've said that before. I might believe you if you didn't always come back.

Good-bye, Jesus.

You didn't fool me.

A heavy dark man hung back in the doorway. "Can I come in?"

"Who are you?" Jesus asked.

"I am Barabbas."

"What can you want with me?"

"Things have gone very badly with me, Jesus. I have come to ask for your help."

"How?"

"As you know, whenever you have been killed, I was spared. When men wanted to revenge themselves on you, they set me free."

"Man is easily distracted," Jesus said.

"But I got the benefit. As long as men were absorbed with you, my crimes were overlooked." The man raised his hand. He was only scratching his head, and Jesus was glad he had not flinched. "Without your distractions, they are judging me very harshly. Faithless rulers don't free me to spite you. And the reverent men who once unchained me as testimony to their beliefs no longer rule governments. I am forever being imprisoned, tortured, even fined."

"And you blame me?"

"If you would bring divine law to men again, they'd be less strict in enforcing their own. I speak for all criminals, Jesus. Bring us mercy in place of justice."

"I thought judges had come to understand that your crimes were not of your choosing. I thought they ruled that you had been marked at birth to be criminals."

"Some men accept that defense," the man said bitterly. "But I'd rather rot in jail than admit I was compelled to be a thief. I did not cast God from my heart to welcome him in my genes."

"You want to be guilty by free choice and freed by happenstance?"

"That was the pattern when you were teaching them to persecute the innocent."

Jesus spoke sharply. "Barabbas is being hanged today in the capital. Who are you?"

The man faltered. "I am Dismas. How did you know?"

"You limp. Barabbas has lurched and crouched, but he's never limped."

"Forgive me."

"My friends sent you? Peter? James?" The man nodded.

"Tell them their sophistry is wasted. Nothing can make me more willing or less helpless."

"You will do what is right, Lord."

"Go away, Dismas. I have nothing to offer you." When the broad back disappeared, Jesus thought about what he had said. I have nothing to offer you. There must be another way, less arrogant, to say it.

Water in their cave had seeped to their bare feet and turned the dirt on their toes to mud. The younger men were in the midst of celebrating the rain, dancing on the soft earth to feel the splatter of mud against their ankles. They were not forgetting as they splashed that their black shirts would be wet now day and night. But their shirts had been damp with sweat for months, and rain at least would be fresher on their backs. They were not forgetting either that the rain might ruin their ammunition and rot their food.

Not forgetting these good reasons for hating the rain, they had begun to cheer when the first torrent of water came crashing out of the sky. They had clapped each other's backs and sung traditional songs of victory. They could rejoice at each burst of a downpour that would leave them filthy and sick because they knew the rain would hurt their enemies even more. The aliens had airplanes, and airplanes could not fly through the mountains in the rain.

"No bombs for three months!" cried James, the merriest boy in the platoon.

"Don't be sure," Peter warned. "They learned to fly at night. They could learn to fly when it rained."

"No!" James shouted. "They may own the skies. But we own the heavens. This rain from heaven is proof we will win."

"You didn't tell us that during the dry months." John spoke from a straw mat at the back of the cave. "You didn't say the sunshine proved that they were going to beat us."

"Of course not! Because they are going to lose. The heavens couldn't send us a false sign, could they?" He swaggered to John's side and put his pistol to his brother's head. "Could they?"

John pushed the barrel aside. "You are right, brother. We are very lucky to have you to sort out the true portents from the false. Otherwise we might come to believe that our winning depends on how bravely we fight."

"Quiet!" In the absence of Jesus, Judas was the commander. "Even if the aliens stay out of the sky, they may come crawling around on foot."

"Especially during the day," John agreed, "when they don't have to be afraid of the dark." The week before, he had been shot in the leg during a daytime scouting foray. When the bullet was dug out of his flesh, he was left with a sore leg and a new distrust of the sun.

"When we rule the country, we will conduct all business at night, to please my brother," James said.

"You have always handled your business at night." The others laughed softly at the bickering between brothers.

"Don't be jealous. They shot low enough. Soon you'll be back at it yourself."

Peter asked Judas when Jesus would rejoin them. He was afraid the question would annoy the acting commander and tried to show in his manner that he was not impatient. "He didn't say."

John had watched Jesus leave three days before, and he told Peter, "He said he was going to get new instructions and didn't know when he'd be back. He expected this week to be quiet because of the holidays."

"How are you going to celebrate?" James kicked his brother's sore leg. "Why don't you dance for us?"

"When I dance, it'll be on your body."

James laughed and danced a parody of John on the battlefield, cowering and cringing, dodging in every direction until at last one bullet catches the very tip of his big toe. Obeying Judas, the men laughed deep in their throats.

One hour passed and then another. At every slight sound the men who could sleep blinked awake. Most of them had grown up on continual alert, and they didn't bother to think that they might be killed at any minute of the day. Older than the others, Peter had known periods of fitful peace, and the tension sometimes told on him. His patience with the clowning of the younger men would break, and during the long daylight hours he would brood and curse their enemies.

The rain stopped for several minutes. Then, as the men were attuning themselves to the silence, the downpour started again with greater force. Outside, the water hit the ground like bomb fragments and stung the face and chest of Andrew, who was standing guard on a ridge thirty feet above the cave. From his post, he could watch the road for more than a mile as it wound through the hills. At an alert from him, the cave's mouth could be barricaded and disguised until no amount of scrutiny would reveal its secret. Only the bombs could hurt them. The alien pilots might hit the hilltop accidentally, dropping with no aim, acting on nothing more than a hunch that guerrillas were camped below.

Andrew had seen the First John, their former leader, buried alive in a cave while the men who could not reach shelter had escaped. The bomber pilot had no way of knowing that he had killed their bravest man. When reports over the traitor radio said the pilot claimed he had killed forty guerrillas, the men of the First John's company did not scoff at his boast. They would have given up forty lives—thirty-nine others and their own—to keep the First John alive.

Later that year Andrew had cut the head off a wounded alien soldier they had captured. Judas and other officers were going to punish him severely until he said, "For the First John." They nodded and kept still.

Andrew wanted the war to end. Like the others, he talked about the blessedness of peace and about the progress the country would make when the shooting had stopped. As he talked, he knew, too, that he didn't want the war to end before he had cut the heads off thirty-nine more alien soldiers. The enemy had set the price. Let them pay it.

Far down the hill Andrew saw something move. After five hours on guard, his eyes sometimes saw more than there was to see. He shut his eyelids for a moment and looked again. Through the heavy rain, a figure was pedaling a bicycle up the road. The rider was a woman. He could see the sodden panel from her long silk dress tied to the bicycle's back bumper to keep it out of the wheel spokes. When she turned right at the next trail, it meant she was coming to the cave. Andrew gave a low whistle, hardly different from a bird's call. Judas appeared at his side.

"Is it Mary Magdalene?" Andrew asked. The sharpness of Judas' eyes was one of their legends.

"She's not supposed to come. There must be trouble in town."

They watched her pedal up the hill until the mud set her tires spinning. She dismounted and hid the bicycle in the tall grass. It took her another ten minutes to struggle the rest of the way. Out of breath, she had to try twice to repeat the sweet bird sound Andrew had made. He dropped down from his hiding place and pulled her into the cave, where Judas was waiting with irritation.

"Why have you come?"

Her eyes were blinking from the darkness, but the men could see her clearly. She was taller than their women, a little darker-skinned and much braver. When the peace had collapsed, she had moved to the province capital to sleep with alien soldiers. Her earnings from the enemy bought food for the guerrillas. To get more cash, she sold on the black market all the presents the aliens gave her. The wives of some rebels said the war had given her an excuse to be the slut she had been destined to become. But they couldn't deny that she had stolen a dozen pistols for their husbands or that she had brought medicine to the cave when they needed it.

Apologetically she said, "I have news. The fourth traitor battalion and the second alien battalion are joining tonight to try to destroy you."

"They don't know where we are."

"They are sending more than a thousand men from here to the river. They are sure they will find you. But I have seen the plans at their headquarters. Only one alien company will pass along here, down the trail by the five rocks. You could surprise them and get back here before the others could relieve them."

Judas thought that one day Mary Magdalene would fall in love with an alien and, as a dowry, would betray her countrymen. Yet her information had been good so far. He listened intently. "You are now a commanding general, are you?" he asked. "You might wish to stay with us and lead the attack yourself since you have planned it so carefully."

"I did not mean to put myself forward." Her meekness, which enchanted the aliens, was genuine. "It was only that as I looked at the maps, it seemed so good a plan. I can draw in the dirt what I saw, and you will find that what I said is nothing more than what any of your soldiers would propose."

"Very well. Draw here." With his toe he scraped clean a square of dirt. Peter put a candle at the center, and James brought a sturdy stick with a sharp point. "Are you sure," Judas asked as she sketched familiar landmarks, "that you saw the actual plan and not a map to mislead spies?"

"The alien colonel keeps it locked in his bedroom. Even the maids in the house do not have a key to the cabinet. They are against us anyway. He has bought their loyalty with money and hair spray." She pulled ruefully at her own damp hair, hanging over her ears like seaweed.

The men who were awake had gathered around her on all sides. With arrows and dotted lines she traced for them the enemy tactics.

"That's good," Judas said when she had finished. "That's good. We can kill more than fifty of their men at little risk."

Philip tried to whisper a question to the girl, but the rain had stopped and everyone in the circle heard him. "Did you bring any chocolate?"

Judas struck him in the face with a closed fist. "She has risked her life to bring us this plan," he said. "Only someone as ungrateful and stupid as you could ask such a thing." Mary Magdalene had moved to caress the sore spot on Philip's cheek, but her pride in Judas' words made her flush.

"We must begin preparing for the ambush," Judas said to her. "You should not be gone any longer. If the aliens find you on the road, you are returning from taking holiday greetings to your family."

"Yes."

Judas waved her away. When she reached the mouth of the cave, he called, "Next time don't forget the chocolate." He gestured impatiently to the men, and they began to wake their comrades. Since they had not fought for nearly two months, they knew Judas would make a ritual of the inspection. Most of their weapons had been captured from the enemy. They were heavy rifles that shot straight and killed efficiently. The men found great satisfaction in shooting an alien soldier with his own bullets.

Last year, when their store of captured ammunition had run low, they had crept to the seacoast. There, from a junk disguised with fishing nets, they had picked up a supply of lighter-weight weapons. Judas knew which large nation had sent the new supplies. But most of the men feared anything outside their province, and he did not tell them they were incurring foreign debts.

Nathanael had begun hauling out the electrically detonated

mines. Watching him, Judas wondered, as he often did, at the inability of his men to learn anything from experience. "Those mines are for limited harassment on the days of enemy convoys," he said, helping Nathanael to put them back beneath a tarpaulin. "Tonight we will not expose our intentions by using mines. You saw the plan the whore drew. We will surround the company between the rocks and the river, and we will kill all of them within two minutes of the first shot we fire. We will give them no warning, and we will leave no trace for their relief forces to follow. Do you understand me?" Nathanael nodded vigorously, too slow and good-humored to detect a reproach.

By the time their rifles had been oiled and their ammunition belts stocked, the rain had ended. The night, darker than the storm, was closing over the hillside. The men had three more hours to wait before taking up their positions, but they did not go back to sleep. They sat silently in the corners of the cave. John, who had not recovered enough to join them in the ambush, knew better than to say a word.

Judas' wristwatch showed less than one hour until they would move out when the bird signal sounded again. He prayed it was not Jesus returning, and he was repeating that prayer when Jesus appeared beside him.

Jesus nodded to the armed men and asked Judas, "Have you had trouble?"

"Not yet." Judas told him every detail of the girl's visit. But as he spoke, he felt that the commander's excitement was not keeping pace with his own. He began to prolong his account, to delay an answer. When he had finished, Jesus said, "The plan is good, but we must cancel it."

They had watched enough men die for Judas to be able to ask, "Why?"

Jesus felt his fingers digging into the softest skin of his palm. He must act calm and firm. "Orders," he said. Judas looked at the captain's shaved head, dusted lightly with bristles of black hair, and tried to decide whether to press him further.

In the past the two of them had spoken of the possibility that a cease-fire would have to be explained one day to their men. Now the holidays could be providing the excuse for politicians in remote cities to begin their negotiations. To them, as to most of the world, the war was a nuisance and an embarrassment.

But to the men in the cave and other men in caves and trenches throughout the country, the war was a religion to be celebrated every night of the year. Telling those men why they must stop killing was a job neither Judas nor Jesus had wanted to take on.

They had agreed that when the moment came, they would be forthright with the men and confess that peace talks might lose all the territory and bargaining strength that the blood of patriots had won for them. They would admit that in another five years they might have to call upon the men to flee to the hills again and begin again to free their country. They would end by saying that they, too, had doubts about the wisdom of negotiating with hypocrites and traitors. But they were good soldiers and the cease-fire was an order. Now, canceling their ambush, Jesus might be acting on that order.

But the shaved head suggested another reason to Judas. In peacetime Jesus had lived contentedly as a priest in the highlands until the traitor government began to torture and kill the nation's religious leaders. Then Jesus had left his lodgings at the temple and joined the First John in his fight for justice. Clever and brave, Jesus had risen quickly through the ranks. But he kept his head shaved, and no one forgot that he had been a priest before he became a soldier.

Only once had Judas argued with his commander. It was not long after he had been sent to the company Jesus led. More truthfully, as Judas recalled it now, he had argued alone; Jesus had heard out his shouting and then overruled him. The issue had been two wounded alien soldiers that they had captured after a long battle. They could not care for the prisoners, and Judas had pulled his pistol, prepared to shoot them.

Jesus stopped him. His god forbade such cruelty, he said. Judas did not share that god, but as a soldier he was bound to obey Jesus. The wounded men were treated and set free.

That was when Judas understood what pain the war was causing the priest. Afterward he shuddered each time Jesus shot an alien, and he looked for ways to comfort him when the fighting was over. If these orders Jesus now brought were from his god, Judas would not quarrel with them. Already the war was a long one. They would have a hundred, a thousand, more chances to kill aliens.

He cast about for a way to show Jesus that, though he did not believe, he could respect the priest's faith. He wanted to convey his loyalty without forcing Jesus to admit that the orders had not come from the province headquarters. Rehearsing his words, Judas sat silently and thought, I am speaking to him in my head, and he can sit beside me and not know what I am telling him. How strange that a slimy thing like a tongue should be the way to go from my head into his.

"There is no one else I want to follow." As Judas spoke, he felt his tongue flick against the roof of his mouth. "I would trust you to interpret our orders, no matter how they came to you."

Knowing the kindness that led him to speak, Jesus almost let his gratitude betray him. He was about to say, "Relieve me of command." But he caught himself and said, "Thank you."

As they waited, his doubts once more began to work on Jesus. He had not heard from an officer at their headquarters. Nor had he heard instructions from his god. Crouched in tall grass, waiting and praying, he had heard from something in his muscle and flesh that said, No more killing.

That was when he should have run away. He could have disappeared into another town or joined the horde of refugees on the road. He had meant to walk away from his troops and vanish from their lives. But he had come back to them with a lie.

Returning to the cave along the hidden paths, Jesus had practiced his argument with Judas:

"I have been alone for three days," he would begin, "and I know we must not fight any more."

"If your god forbids it, you should not join us," Judas would answer. "He has come to see the justice of our cause before, and he will release you to us again."

"My conviction does not come from my god. He has not spoken to me for many months."

"Then without regret you can join us in the cause of freedom."

"I am telling you that we must not kill. We must lay down our arms."

"When our land is overrun by aliens who would enslave us, one course lies open to honorable men. If our leader—or if your god—directs us to stop our struggle, I will obey. But any other voice with the same order is a voice of cowardice and treachery, and I will never surrender."

Jesus knew their argument would have been longer and finally harsher than he was imagining it. Judas could repeat each of the brave old words eloquently, and he believed the words as he spoke them. In their argument, Jesus could not speak with that same conviction, for Jesus knew he was wrong. God had not told him to lay down his arms. God watched the aliens murdering farmers, setting fire to the rice crop, torturing prisoners to make them betray their countrymen. God watched, and if he was God, he would not ask godly men to let an alien plague destroy their land.

But if there was no God, then Jesus would have to listen

to his own soft instincts, to the numbness that crept across his body saying, No more killing.

Jesus said to himself, I am wrong. That I had to lie proves it. Anyone can laugh at the fine words Judas likes to speak, but they are fine because they are true. Yet my body says, No more killing. I have seldom listened to my body, but I cannot ignore it now.

Judas said, "We will take the men out anyway. There would be too much danger for the wounded if we stay here. We will follow the same route, if you approve, but we will not open fire unless they engage us."

"We are not to fire at all."

"Surely your instructions don't forbid self-defense?"

After a pause Jesus said, "No."

"There should be no need for shooting." Judas' excitement was rising in him again like mercury. "We will be well concealed, and they will march through the site without detecting us."

"Good."

"I would suggest one thing." Judas was sure that the nearness of the aliens would overcome Jesus' scruples and that the ambush could proceed. If later it turned out that the orders had actually come from their headquarters, some excuse could be made. Violations were an expected counterpoint to a cease-fire.

"What do you suggest?"

"If you would take a command spot at the top of the west ridge, you could survey the valley. At any change in the aliens' plans, you could alert us with two shots when they have passed you. We would then spread out and let them chase a few men to the river. The rest could pick up the wounded and move to the old cave." Two shots, Judas thought, and we will have our battle. You will find that a commander gives his best orders with his trigger finger.

Jesus was glad to be spared the company of other men during the long wait, and he agreed at once.

"We must begin soon," Judas said. "They will be out shortly before dawn, and we should be concealed before midnight."

With a few brusque motions, Judas grouped the men into small units and gave them instructions. Unless they heard the signal from Jesus, they were not to open fire. The reasons for this order were good ones. They would have to accept the word of their commanders. No one grumbled and the older men looked relieved.

Judas led out the groups separately. For more than an hour he ran between the cave and the rim of the natural bowl that seemed shaped to be an ambush site. Jesus had filled his canteen from the rain barrel and was setting out for his post when Judas caught up with him. "Sir!"

"Yes?"

"We have to do things that are wrong," Judas said softly. "Killing is never right, but sometimes we must do it."

Jesus answered, "We have all killed at one time or another."

Judas wanted to comfort him now for the slaughter to come. "I never try to persuade myself that killing is right. But the world is wrong, and it forces wrongdoing on us."

"We are the world."

"What I wanted to say was that I don't deceive myself. I know it's wrong, even when it must be done." Judas dropped away soundlessly and Jesus continued his climb to the ridge.

The nights were cold in the hills. Dressed in black silk shirt and trousers, Jesus trembled from every wind that blew through the hollows. He tried to huddle low enough for the rough grass to cover him. In front he pushed down the underbrush until he could see along the trail the aliens were expected to follow.

Jesus, never outside his province, feared all aliens, and he knew his troops shared his fear. The enemy could swoop from the sky like eagles, jump out of green flying trucks and fight until those trucks lifted them out of the jungle and back to their bases. The men asked Jesus why his god should have given such power to the aliens. He said that God had given to the loyal soldiers strong hearts and great skill and, to make them test these gifts, a heartless enemy with a million machines.

When he had stood watch on this ridge in the summer, Jesus could often hear all the noises of the village below. This night the rain had left behind a thick vapor that swallowed the lights below him and smothered any sound of life. He was reminded of nights at the temple school when young boys strained to carry in tubs of hot water, and the novices, blushing to be naked, crouched in the steam, hiding and cleaning themselves. In the night fog, Jesus shivered from that same nakedness, but he felt neither hidden nor clean. He thought, If we are to save our souls, we should not be asked to save our country.

Jesus considered the paths Judas straddled. As a soldier, Judas could kill. As a man, he could not. And so he tried to lay down his manhood each time he took up his rifle. Even that compromise could not save Jesus tonight. He had climbed this ridge as a soldier, and now he was going to refuse to kill. I know I am wrong, he thought. I can share that much courage with Judas. I won't pretend that I am right.

The spike-edged grass bore into his back. He shifted silently to blunt the pressure of its blades. Some men loved to sit in this tall grass at night, digging their fingers into the soil and dreaming of the day they would return to their farms. All his life Jesus had been different. He preferred to be inside a temple with its incense and its traces of poppy smoke from the pipes of dying priests. He had liked the daytime when he could be with other men, reading under a roof. And he found himself alone in the grass at night.

His passion had been spent during the three days of futile prayer. It was halfheartedly now that Jesus asked his god, Tell me that I am not to kill. Your command would wipe away my fear and cowardice. Even Judas could accept my betrayal. God, I pray to you: Sanctify my treason.

He expected no answer and got none.

Usually the aliens struck shortly before dawn. In that way they could summon their aircraft at the first light and pursue the guerrillas with rockets and bombs. But from the look of the sky, the morning sun would be lost in a fog that would hold the planes on the ground. In five hours Judas and the others could be back in the cave, alive and with their rifles unfired. He worried for nothing.

When Jesus had been downhearted in the past, he comforted himself with a vision of the country in twenty years' time, after the guerrillas had freed the capital and restored peace. He had imagined the schoolchildren in his own village —they would be the children of those same infants he now saw being carried around the market—at desks in a clean modern school. They would be reading about this unreal war and memorizing the names of the First John and the other heroes.

For those children, the studying would be a chore. Even the boys who learned to respect the First John could never know that he had been a cursing loud man who swaggered under the weight of his gun belt and needed freedom the way other men need food.

Whenever he had pictured the school, the idea of young faces untroubled by war or hunger had touched him. This night he found himself resenting their bored looks as they read about the great war. If he could not rouse himself tonight, his name might appear in their books as a traitor. They'd learn of him as a man who falsified his orders and risked the lives of the men he led. Sitting in snug classrooms, they would not hear his body cry, No more killing. They would believe that he had been a coward. If the writer of their book said Jesus had taken money from the aliens to lay down his arms, they would believe that.

It is not just. I must live in the world, but I will be judged by scholars, who have avoided life, writing for children, who have not begun to live. Something is lost. Life is lost. The cry of my body is lost. And a generation of children will sneer or spit when they speak my name.

Four hours had passed before Jesus detected in the distance the first dull sound of movement. The aliens tried so hard for silence that they made a noise like nothing else in the jungle. Instead of creeping steadily with a rustling that might have been the wind, they moved in stealthy short bursts, and their step shook the earth like the beat of a bass drum.

The thumping had become louder. Jesus stretched to see if the red pinpoints of their cigarettes were burning through the darkness. He saw no lights. Their discipline meant they were older and better-trained aliens who would be less easy to elude.

A scout from the first unit appeared on the trail about fifty feet from where Jesus hid. The overcast moon revealed nothing but a dim profile that reminded Jesus again of the aliens' great size. The man stood a full foot taller than Jesus, and the muscle of his arm looked as big around as Jesus' waist.

As the man moved forward, raising a leg, setting it down, Jesus saw others behind him. His own heart had begun to beat loudly, and he wondered, as once he had wondered when he played a child's hiding game, if the pounding in his chest could carry to his enemies. He knew better, and he thought, Our fear speaks only to us. Unless we tell them, the men around us never have to know that we're afraid.

Every one of the aliens was huge. Peter said their forefathers had spread their seed among apes, and that all aliens were half beast. John said they merely ate more than other people and that the patriots would defeat them with the weapons of hunger and privation. It had been Thomas who said what they all had considered: The aliens were gods whom the patriots had no right to resist. Soon afterward, Thomas had been killed in the confusion of a battle.

As he watched them pass, Jesus saw that the men were moving four abreast across the clearing rather than in the pairs Judas had expected. There would be twice as many men on the mission, then, and the aliens could fan out in patterns that the girl had not charted. Moving around Judas' trap instead of through its center, these men could surround the patriots and gun them down.

Jesus knew he had to warn his comrades. He held his rifle ready to fire the signals that would send the patriots scattering to safety. He could fire the shots, dart through the brush and join them at the old cave.

The gun butt weighed on his palm. Its thin barrel rose out of the grass like a burnt stalk. He laid his finger across the trigger. But his fingers did not tighten and he knew he would not fire.

Cowardice said: Judas will see that he is outmaneuvered and outmanned, and he will keep the men silent until he can lead them back to the cave.

Fear said: Warning shots will set off a slaughter, and you will emerge from this hiding place to find a dead body in every clump of grass.

His body said: No more killing.

Jesus put his rifle down.

Cowardice said: If you shoot, you will guarantee a massacre, for the aliens will pursue your men and kill them all. This way, as long as Judas obeys your instructions, they are safe. You have betrayed no one. You have chosen prudence and caution. Since you have done nothing, you are blameless.

Jesus asked himself: Why is cowardice despised when it is such a friend of man? Why is bravery esteemed when it offers only pain and death?

The aliens had passed, and the silence of the mountains surrounded Jesus again. He heard nothing but the low voice of his body speaking through his pulse.

Then, so soft and muffled that it might have been a trick of his ears, a shot was fired. The next barrage was thunder, Jesus told himself, but the sky did not light up. Each new burst of bullets came faster, and the sounds of gunfire crossed each other until no single rifle could be heard. The crashing carried through the hills to Jesus and rocked him with its force.

He felt his face twisting with fear. In the midst of the din from the valley, he listened for the reassurance of his body. But a tremor shook him, and it said, Kill! He sat in the grass and knew about betrayal.

Not long after the shooting had stopped, an alien soldier turned a beam of light across the ridge and spotted Jesus in the underbrush. He shouted something that must have meant, "Come out!" Jesus rose, leaving his rifle in the grass. He folded his hands behind his head and joined the alien on the path.

The soldier grunted and prodded Jesus down the hill with the tip of his rifle barrel. As he obeyed, Jesus had no thoughts in his head. He saw that the fog was lifting, after all, and that the dawn was not far off. The beauty of the dark hills etched itself on his vision for an instant and was gone.

When they approached the ambush site, Jesus began to see the bodies of the men. They had fallen into the grass, and he saw only a leg or an arm. If a hand was large and luminous, it belonged to an alien. Even in death the guerrillas fitted better into the landscape. Once he tripped on the body of a loyalist who had been caught on the path when the shooting had begun. He steadied himself with a hand on the thin chest of a comrade he could not identify. Behind him, the alien profited from his stumble and walked around the corpse.

The light, when it came, came quickly. By the time the guard ordered Jesus to stop, the sun was strong enough to make them both blink. The alien smoked a cigarette. Jesus, who did not smoke, was glad the guard did not offer one to him, for he was not sure how to refuse. All his life he had been polite, and now there was something ugly about politeness.

They waited a long time. The alien soldier was talking to himself, taking only a few puffs on his cigarette, throwing it to the ground, grinding it under his boot, lighting another. Jesus thought how the waste would hurt John, who loved to smoke and rarely got the chance. John would be safe with the other wounded men in the cave. The girl would bring them food.

As the waiting dragged on, Jesus wondered why the nervous alien did not shoot him there. He must be an underling who had to get orders from his commander. Jesus understood why the alien government had sent soldiers to his country, but he looked at his guard and wondered why the soldiers had agreed to come. The man was tanned except around the eyes, where he had worn dark glasses. There, under his pale eyelashes, the skin was brown and purple from fatigue. He must have a reason, Jesus thought. He must believe he is fighting for something.

My cause is just, and I betrayed it. His cause is false, and he has kept its faith.

Three men drew close to them. One was a tall alien, no different from the man who guarded Jesus; another was a traitor, hurrying along like a hungry dog at the alien's heels; the third was Peter, marching forward at the point of the alien's gun.

The guard with Jesus approached his alien comrade respectfully, said something and gestured toward Jesus. The alien commander came closer to inspect the new prisoner.

Jesus looked into his eyes and saw that their lids were skinned back in a way he recognized. After other battles, the loyal soldiers who survived had returned to the cave with eyes thrust open in the same way. After a day had passed, the lids drew down and became a shield again. Until that blankness in their eyes was covered, Jesus had turned away from their faces.

Now he thought: We have always recognized the aliens by their height and color and the odd shape of their eyelids. But this morning the commander's stare makes him kin to every soldier he has killed. I with my narrow eyes have become the alien.

Speaking the liquid sounds of his alien language, the commander said something to the traitor, who translated it to Peter. "Do you know this man?" the traitor asked, pointing to Jesus.

"I have never seen him before," Peter said contemptuously.

"He is part of your company of outlaws," the translator insisted.

"Our company had only brave men."

"You lie. He is one of yours."

"Only the traitor slaves of aliens lie. I tell you my friends are dead. But our cause will triumph."

"Shut your mouth."

The traitor relayed Peter's denial to the commander. He spoke fluently in the alien tongue, the natural manliness of his own voice sinking into a soft whine. Twice he pointed to Jesus and once he drew his pistol, but the commander shook his head and turned his wide blank eyes to the ground.

Jesus knew he would not be killed.

The traitor came back to him with a look of revulsion. "You!" he said. When Jesus did not respond, he said, "Pig!" Jesus lifted his head.

"The allied commander refuses to shoot you as you deserve," the traitor said. "He says that if you had been with the others you would have warned them. He says there is no evidence against you.

"They have the weapons, our allies, but they have no cour-

age. We must forever show them the way for real men to be-
have. If we were alone, I would cut off your tongue, so you
would lie no more. I would rip out your eyes so you might
begin to see how your outlaws are destroying this country."

Jesus' head drooped, and the traitor slapped him hard to
raise it. The sound made the alien commander look back and
speak sharply.

"He says, 'No brutality,' " the traitor said bitterly. "Can
you understand any soldier who must fight your kind of ver-
min saying, 'No brutality'?"

His dark eyes searched Jesus for a last time. "I am letting
you go. But as you run off, remember that I might forget my
orders and shoot you in the back. You'd better run fast and
keep running, for if I ever see you again, I will shoot out your
heart."

Jesus walked away. The light was sharp and he began to
recognize faces on the bodies he came upon in the grass.
From one corpse the back of the head had been blown off,
and gray juices from inside his skull were soaking into the
ground. It was Judas.

Jesus knelt by the body and took the cracked head in his
arms. He cupped his palm to scoop the fluid from the earth.
Dirt had mixed with the juices, and Jesus packed this mud into
the wound. He took off his own black shirt and wrapped it
tightly around the head so none of the juice could run out
again. With his head swathed in black, Judas looked sinister,
and whole. Jesus, with no place to go, started to walk faster.

Luke had devised a new version of the parable. In it, the
prodigal son preferred to starve to death rather than humiliate
himself by seeking his father's pardon. Jesus read the story
and tore it up.

Then Luke produced an ending in which the prodigal son

tried to return home but found that his family had moved to a destination unknown to the neighbors. Jesus tore up what Luke had shown him.

"We need a new ending," Luke pleaded. "In the classrooms they're no longer interested in the original story."

"Then write about a starving beggar who imagines in his delirium that pride had once driven him to leave his father's fine estate. Let his hunger cause him to believe that he has returned to that unreal house and that he has been welcomed with love and banquets."

"Is that the end?"

"At the height of the delirium, let him be visited by a traveler who breaks into his fantasy and convinces him that the house, the father, the fatted calf are all lies, and that he is dying ignored and alone."

"We cannot call it the story of the prodigal son."

"Call it the story of the Samaritan."

"The Good Samaritan?"

"Let your students worry about that."

A warning: If I survive without you and learn to pass the days without straining for your voice, then I will never listen to you afterward. Then if you come to me and say, "It will be again as it has been," I will tell you, "No." I will tell you that I wanted to progress in faith, and you denied that progress to me. If I progress now in doubt, my success may disgust me. But my progress will be undeniable. A warning.

John had come to Jesus to say, "There is one miracle after all: knowing another body better than you know your own."

Two mornings later, John returned. "But I have learned from you. I will not try to turn a miracle into a religion."

They had walked all over the old city until they found themselves at the biggest of the mosques, a pile of red sandstone not very different from the famous fort. Heat on Sunday seemed worse than on weekdays, and Jesus felt sun searing his long hair. In two months he was going to be fifty, and he had stopped thinking about a message from God. John was with him.

Their guide had opened an ornate wooden door at one end of the gallery. To enter, they had to duck below a string decked with bits of cloth—offerings from the city's poor. "We did better than a few old rags," Jesus told John.

"They are destitute here."

The guide said, "This is a hair from the head of the prophet." A very coarse hair was taped to a glass slide. "You see it is the color of ginger. That was his color. The hair is fourteen hundred years old."

"From A.D. 600?" Jesus asked. The day before, he had quarreled with some Hindus about the designation "B.C." "From the year 600?" John corrected him, and the guide nodded before ducking again into a dark closet.

"This is the footprint of the prophet," the man said, thrusting a piece of marble before them. "It was a miracle. When the prophet stepped on the marble, it melted and left this impression."

John said, before Jesus could say anything, "That's at least the same."

"Is it the imprint we saw here before?"

"It is. The hair is new. But that's the same slab. This place had been finished a year or two before we got here. You didn't like it."

"The color has faded. It's better now."

Their guide disappeared inside. Jesus knew that John was worried about him and waited until the man was gone before he began to mock the relics. "I think that print is the one I made for a theater."

"Of course not. This one is marble. I remember it."

"It looks wider than my foot."

"It wasn't yours. Don't you remember?"

"I'm an old man, John. A shaky old man. A disgusting, repellent, lazy, hopeless old man. Keep that in mind."

"I only said hopeless. I can't believe you couldn't—"

"I can't. You'll have to accept what I tell you. What about the footprint?"

John liked to reminisce, and he drew Jesus to the pool at the center of the mosque. "You remember Stephen?"

"Vaguely." Out of the shade, Jesus' head began to throb. He wanted John to be quick, but they had not had much to say to each other during the trip, and he also wanted to prolong this talk.

"One of the seven. Stephen."

"I know." Jesus laughed, a sound he didn't like. "He was always in trouble. Why, do you suppose? He would do the same things or say the same things as I would do or say. And they loved me and despised him."

John went on, "Stephen was with us that time. Not here, but not far. I forget. A little south, as I recall."

"Yes."

"You were sick, or that's what we called it then. You wouldn't move. We had a tent for you, and you lay in there all day. You wouldn't come out. You wouldn't eat. You were surly and rude to everyone."

"That's right. Mother had come to see me—"

"Your poor mother. That was a long trip in those days. She stuck her head in the tent and you threw something at her."

"A rose."

"A rose," John snorted. "It left a welt. You were as bad as

I'd ever seen you. And all the time plans were going ahead
for the ceremony. We hoped you'd pull out of it in time."

"Something like now."

All the zest went out of John. "No, then you were part of
it. We could get you over the bad times."

"Now it's all bad times?"

"Let me go on. There you were in your tent. Not moaning.
Not saying anything. Just lying on the rugs and staring at the
tent pole. The day came, and you were no better. We were
panic-stricken. Thousands of people were supposed to hear
you, and then they were to witness a miracle afterward."

"The marble."

John flushed. "The wax. We were dealing with very simple
people. They would listen, but the footprint would convince
them. Anyway, we finally settled on Stephen. They had seen
the rest of us, but he was new to the camp and an imposing
figure."

"Fat."

John let it pass. "We started with the prayer, and that
went smoothly. Then Stephen lit into Judaism, and that puzzled most of the people. Oh, only about two thousand had
shown up."

"Stephen was never the draw I was."

John laughed, a sound they both liked. He rose and they
walked together down the faded red stairs to the street. "We
took the imprint of his foot in wax and substituted the marble block we had prepared. For an hour, we prayed and sang
over the miracle. As we were ready to send everyone home, a
few of the elders came forward and started putting questions
to Stephen: What may we eat and drink? How many wives
can a man have? What is heaven like? Well, you know
Stephen."

"Not really."

"He answered them. Paul was there, biting his tongue. It
was wonderful. I've never seen anyone so angry."

"I've been spared Paul's wrath."

"To your face. So there was Stephen, talking off the top of his head about four wives. And Paul, who believes castration is too good for most people, knotting his hands and clearing his throat and pulling his beard. He tried afterward to explain away Stephen's speech. But it was too late. They'd found a Messiah more to their taste."

Jesus looked back at the mosque, warm red in the late sun. "Does anyone see Stephen now?"

"He dropped out of sight. Somebody saw him later and said he insisted on being called by the name they'd given him."

"Delusions. The occupational hazard."

"Where shall we go now?"

"Back to the hotel?"

John stepped off the curb to find a taxi. He was glad he had made up the story. The session with the Hindus had taught him that things were bad enough now without the old jealousies.

Mary Magdalene asked, "Is there anything I can do?"

"No," he said.

"What's the noise outside, James?"

"It's Thomas, Lord. He insists on seeing you."

"I'm seeing no one."

"We told him that. The men are struggling with him."

"Why is he so insistent?"

"He doesn't believe that you have been let loose by God. He thinks you're trying to hoard redemption for yourself. He says he is being cheated."

"He doubts my loss?"

"Yes, Lord."

"What wounds can I show him, James?"

"Show him your eyes, Lord."

"I don't weep now."

"Show him your dry eyes."

"I don't hear anything in the corridor. He must be gone."

"Yes."

"Will he go on feeling cheated?"

"I think he will."

"Lucky Thomas. Isn't that right, James?"

"Yes, Lord."

"Wipe your eyes, James, or leave the room."

"I'm leaving, Lord."

"Wipe your eyes."

"No."

"Is that Thomas back?"

"No, Lord, it's a group of students."

"And?"

"They've signed a petition. It says they love you, no matter whose son you are. They love your gentleness and tolerance and humility. They want you to know that they don't care if you're God or not, they will never forget you."

"Tell them they were very gentle, tolerant and humble to come here today."

"I'll thank them for you."

The pressure within his head, an alien weight, gave him a pleasure he was afraid to admit. Jesus prayed, Don't let me come to love cancer because it is an outside force that can destroy me. Let me be truer than that to my better days.

"I want to talk a cross," Jesus said to Matthew. "Show me how to do it."

"I don't understand, Lord."

"I want to lie here and build a cross with words. Then I want to climb up and hang myself on it."

"You can't do that."

"I know I can't. I want you to help me."

"No one can do that with words. You can't make a cross with words."

"Then they're no good, are they?"

"Lord?"

"Words are no good."

"Not for making a cross. There are other things they can make."

"Don't be a fool, Matthew."

"No, Lord."

"If we can't talk a cross, why are you climbing up with your arms flung apart?"

"I don't understand, Lord."

"Don't you feel the nails?"

"Are you saying something to hurt me, Lord?"

"Come down, Matthew."

"Lord?"

"Climb down."

"I believe that you're the Son of God," the young man told him with sincerity. Jesus had not slept for many days and felt too tired to question him. His face was unfamiliar, but it might be a new Nathanael who had found him here.

"Take me home."

"I sleep here," Jesus said.

"Give me money for coffee."

Jesus reached into his pocket and pulled out a few coins. The man snatched them all, jumped from the bench and ran into the shadows. "I would have given them to you," Jesus called. "I have a few more." He dug far into his pants for the rest of his money. "You could have had these. If you needed it, you should have told me." He found that he was talking to himself and stopped. It worried him that he talked to himself. Now I should be rich, he thought, keeping his mouth closed. At least I could give them money. I would have money to give.

JESUS: Guess what's more debasing than to believe in something that never existed.

SIMON: What?

JESUS: To stop believing in something that never existed.

Jesus thought, If bombs fell tomorrow, I would not be a failure.

JESUS: Guess what's the most romantic idea.

PETER: That men wanted to reform their lives?

JESUS: That's the second most romantic idea.

PETER: What's first?
JESUS: That I wanted them to.

Summoned early in the afternoon, Thaddaeus didn't appear
until after the tea table had been cleared and the other disciples had left for the evening. He entered the common room
with a casualness Jesus decided was not natural to him. Tall
and dark, with cheeks sourly sucked into his jaws, Thaddaeus
was almost unknown to the rest of the men. Jesus had been
put off by his sulky Northern accent, but he wished he had
tried harder with him. Looking at those sunken cheeks, he
knew his regrets had come too late.

"Sit down," Jesus said easily. "Would you care for some
wine?"

"I don't drink." Thaddaeus managed to sound both aggrieved and self-righteous.

"A glass now and then might be good for your digestion.
You have gas, don't you?"

"My stomach's not what it should be. I'm in pain a lot of
the time. Of course, that rich food here don't help me. But
when I ask the cook for more junkets and puddings, he gets
uppity."

"I'll see if we can't arrange a blander diet for you. The
chef has a professional pride that I encourage without understanding."

"He just stirs up a mess of food. It's nothing so special
to do."

"I agree with you. But he can do it, and none of the rest
of us can, so we'll probably go on making allowances for his
temper."

"I'd give him the sack and let everyone eat out of tins."

"Then I'm afraid they'd all have gas. But that's not why I

asked you to stop by. Peter tells me you've been hearing from God."

"That's right." Thaddaeus brushed back his lank hair and set his face to meet the accusation.

"You know I am very interested in this development," Jesus continued, "since for some time my own communication with God has been infrequent. I was a little surprised that you didn't come to me as soon as this experience began."

Jesus watched the young man calculating whether he should risk being brazen. Apparently he decided he could not carry it off, for he lowered his eyes and nearly cringed. "I didn't want to cause trouble."

"How could contact with God cause trouble?"

"Well, I knew you were feeling badly about the way things had been going, and I thought you might not take it kindly if—"

"You thought I'd resent God's show of favoritism?"

Thaddaeus was feeling more sure of himself, and he looked up at Jesus appraisingly, with a flicker of malice behind his eyes. "It'd be only natural."

"That was the reason, then, that you suggested to Peter that the others all be informed of your blessedness?"

"I thought they should know."

"And the elections?"

Thaddaeus knew that to stumble now would be fatal. He plunged ahead. "It seemed to some of us that we should have more choice in naming our leaders, and an election seemed the fairest way."

"Did God suggest an election?"

"I don't want to talk about my messages from God. Anyone can say whatever he likes and then claim he heard it from God."

"Quite true." Jesus had decided in advance not to bicker.

"The election idea seemed to appeal to most of the others.

Of course the details haven't been worked out yet."

"Do you suggest a campaign? What would be the opposing platforms?"

Thaddaeus began to elaborate, and Jesus knew he was hearing phrases practiced on the other men. "There'd be only one issue, naturally: Who is best fitted to carry out God's will."

"The test would be: Who has God last spoken to? It seems to me your plan encourages a hectic kind of competition. Surely God stands for something more than mode or whim?"

"That's what I thought, too. But then it came to me—" he was pleased by the equivocal phrase—"that God wasn't some musty page out of an old book either. He had the right to point new directions for us."

"Along with new leaders."

Thaddaeus licked his lips delicately, liked the taste and licked again. "I'm not in any way pushing for myself. I know how unworthy I am. Any one of the others is better educated or has finer manners or seems to be more of a gentleman. But for some reason or other, God has taken to talking to me. I may be pitiful and all that, but I've got to do as God tells me."

"I would not argue, Thaddaeus, with anything you've said."

As he began to see that he might be granted his demand, Thaddaeus was shifting slightly in his chair. He straightened his shoulders slightly and leaned forward until his posture, to Jesus, looked supplicating. "Then you think what I've suggested is a good idea?"

If I cannot be God's son, Jesus thought, I can be kind enough to spare this boy a supremacy he fears. "I think it's inevitable."

"We could form a committee to set a date for the vote," Thaddaeus suggested.

"An election would be an empty formality. Instead, I shall call a meeting at which anyone may speak. I shall tell the others what they already know: that God has ended all communion with me. You can then reveal to them what God has told you, and you will become the leader."

"I will become Jesus Christ?" For an instant, greediness for the title crowded out his uncertainty.

"We are far too advanced in our belief to suppose that God's favor resides in any one name. You will be Thaddaeus. Whether you become Christ is, after all, between you and God."

"All right," said Thaddaeus, disappointed but with no rebuttal.

"I must confess that I look forward to hearing what you have refused to tell me."

"What do you mean?"

"I'll rejoice to hear the voice of God again, even though I'm no longer his instrument."

Thaddaeus strained forward in the leather chair. "I've told you that I can't tell anyone what God has said to me. I will swear to the others that God spoke, but I couldn't—I won't —say anything more than that."

Jesus relaxed further into the springs of his chair as Thaddaeus pressed near. "You must see," Jesus said, "that to share God's word will be your single duty. Many men had heard God, but I came forward and told what I had heard, even when every instinct warned me to keep God's message hidden in my heart."

"I can't do it."

At the anguished look on Thaddaeus' face, Jesus felt a flash of his own past doubts and pain. "You must."

Thaddaeus flung himself out of his chair to embrace Jesus' legs and sob into the rough fabric of his rumpled trousers. "I can't," he repeated. "I've almost gotten what I wanted, and now I can't do it. I can't."

"There's no disgrace," Jesus said, patting perfunctorily at the boy's shoulder. "God doesn't expect everyone to have the strength. Take comfort from being chosen to hear his word. That should be enough."

Thaddaeus raised his sly face, stained with tears. "No," he said. "No, it's not enough for me. It's not what I wanted."

Jesus stopped patting him and rested his hand on the arm of the chair. *He thinks I've defined his duties in a way that will exclude him. He thinks I saved myself by denying him his chance for glory. He hates me.*

"I'm afraid, Thaddaeus," Jesus said, "that you had better learn to believe it's what you wanted."

What have I learned?

That what men call goodness is nothing more than a search for pain. That what they call evil is the inflicting of pain.

Two brief lessons, only long enough to threaten my existence.

Rising again, I ask myself, Can I live if they don't eat my flesh? Can I die if they won't drink my blood?

Philip had found the old house on the day it nearly burned to the ground. He was drawn there by the sirens of four fire trucks rushing to stop the flames before they spread to more costly homes downwind on the beach.

As he watched firemen chop their way from room to room, Philip could see that the house had been deserted for months before the fire erupted in a downstairs bedroom. He asked bystanders if they knew who owned the building. Later he explained to Peter that he had not expected to find the owner reeking of gasoline or trailing matches. But he had assumed that if the landlord lived anywhere nearby, the disaster would have brought him to the scene.

When none of the neighbors could identify the owner,

Philip began to consider the sanctuary that a rent-free house could provide for thirteen men, three women and a child. By the next day, Simon, Martha and Matthew had been named a delegation to join Philip for an inspection of the three-story building. Their guide forgot momentarily that he was case-hardened and cynical, and he drenched them with enthusiasm for the project. "For heaven's sake, Philip," Martha finally protested. "You sound more like a real estate agent than a newspaper reporter."

"I don't care if we move here or not." He slid easily back to form. "I doubt that we'll find anything more suitable. But I certainly don't care either way. If you don't like this place, we can stay scattered throughout the city and spend the rest of our lives on buses."

Picking his way over the damp ashes, Simon had set out to count the toilets. He was soon back; there were two. Martha found the kitchen awkward and cramped, and Matthew detected evidence of termites in the foundation.

"But look at the full basement," Philip protested. "You know how rare they are near the ocean. Judas could have the whole thing for his tubes and burners. We'd never have to see him."

"At least," Matthew joked, "the rent is right."

Simon, a volunteer welfare worker, remained dubious. "I hand over charity every day," he said, "to people who live in better places than this." But when they voted, he agreed to make their recommendation unanimous.

Philip had discovered the house. It was Andrew's job to hide it again. He boarded the windows on all three floors, and he plastered the outside walls with red warning signs. On the south and east, he cited health regulations; on the west and north, the building and safety code. When the work was done, passers-by would believe that loitering near the premises exposed them to falling beams and smallpox.

One side door was nailed around the frame in a way that

let its center panel swing free. Otherwise every entrance into the house was blocked. Old Mary pronounced the result cozy. Jimmy called it a prison, and they couldn't deny his authority to make the comparison. But everyone agreed that a free house was worth some inconvenience.

Their poet, John, demanded and got one uncovered window in the attic. He reached his porthole by climbing two flights of stairs and grappling with a homemade ladder. Once aloft, he could watch the waves lapping a few hundred feet from their locked door.

Young Mary's child was the only other member of their group to share John's fever for the ocean. But any time the boy joined John in the attic, his mother paced the floor and rattled drawers in the bedroom below them. "I think your mother is looking for you, Laz. You'd better hustle down and see what she wants." At five years old, the boy obeyed perfectly, slipping away with a smile.

Within a week or two they had settled completely into the house and could not believe they had ever lived separately in bungalow courts and cheap hotels. Andrew had installed his machinery with a minimum of carpentry and replastering. Judas moved crates of delicate equipment into the basement without breaking a flask.

"It's comfortable here," Nathanael told Martha one day. "I never expected to have a room of my own to study in."

"Does that mean your grades will improve?"

Nathanael was unshamed. "I don't suppose they will. Next week we're marching at the courthouse every day, and on Mondays, Wednesdays and Fridays our steering committee meets at the union. I've tried studying on the bus. But now that we're so much closer to the campus, I find my place in the book and it's time to get off."

"When I was young, we went to school to learn," Martha said. "We weren't so sure we already knew everything."

Nathanael smiled in a way that showed his chipped front

tooth. He had learned to smile with his mouth shut, but Martha said the tight line of his lips made him look smug. "Not everything. Just more than—"

"We do?"

Nathanael nodded his curly head. "After all, that's progress. I don't know why you old people should be so surprised." He ducked the hand she raised to swat him.

"Jesus would like it if you did well at school." She had no writ for the statement. She didn't know any more what Jesus thought.

"Jesus says men have to choose between doing good and doing well."

"That sounds more like Philip to me."

Nathanael rubbed his chin where scraping off his thick whiskers had left a permanent rash. "Then Jesus inspired him to say it."

"You have an answer for everything, don't you?"

"It's the age, old woman. We live in an age of answers, and that seems to make old folks more nervous than all the centuries of doubt and ignorance."

"Out of the mouths of babes ofttimes comes baby talk," she said snappishly.

"What was that?" demanded a voice from the loudspeaker by the old gas stove.

"I was repeating a proverb," Martha said into the speaker.

"You'll have to speak up," the voice said. "There's a short in one of the wires, and I'm not picking up either the kitchen or the dining room loudly enough to record."

"All right, Andrew."

"What?"

"I said all right."

"Thank you."

"It's a nuisance, isn't it?" she asked Nathanael.

The boy moved close enough to the speaker that he wouldn't have to raise his voice. "Just the same, Andrew's come a long way. When I was growing up, I had to write down a copy of everything I said. I'm amazed now that I said anything at all. Lazarus doesn't remember any of that. He doesn't know how lucky he is."

"Yes," she agreed. "The young ones are never appreciative."

Nathanael was suddenly serious. "You know, that's bothered a lot of us—remembering that to boys Lazarus' age we're going to seem as outdated as Peter seems to me. We talked at one meeting about trying to figure out what's going to bother boys that age when they grow up, so we could start doing something now."

"Leave them their own chance to make fools of themselves," Martha said. "We've done that much."

"It makes me feel as though anything we can do now is already obsolete."

From the oven Martha pulled a large lopsided cake. "If I was supposed to spend my life in a kitchen," she said, "why couldn't I have been given the talent? I almost persuade myself it's the fault of the stove, and then John comes in and whips up a perfect soufflé."

Young Mary had burst into the kitchen in time to wince at John's name. "Ecce would like soufflés, wouldn't he?" she asked. "Anything airy."

"I've been hoping to see you," Nathanael said. Young Mary considered him too boyish to hold any promise for her. But her eyes played over him as he talked, and she let her tongue sneak out to wet her lips. "Of course you have," she said. "If I were a man, I'd crouch by the stairs for hours to get a good look at my legs. I'm the best-looking woman you'll ever meet. Why shouldn't you hope to see me?"

"That's not what I meant."

"Why isn't it? Sometimes, Natty, I think you're as bad as John."

"Just listen to me for a minute. I've found a nursery rhyme for Laz."

"Oh, have you, Nat?" Mary clutched his arm. "Oh, I take

it all back. There's nothing wrong with you at all."

"I told an instructor of mine that you wouldn't let your son hear anything with hatred or violence. He came up with this." Nathanael took a notebook page from his pocket and read:

> There was an old woman
> Lived under a hill;
> And if she's not gone,
> She lives there still.

Nathanael passed the paper to Mary, who examined it suspiciously. "You can't object to that," he said. "It's totally harmless. It even instills an elementary respect for logic."

"Just a minute!" Mary skipped out of the kitchen and up the stairs to the room she shared with Martha and old Mary.

"She'll find something wrong with it," Martha said. "I suggested Jack Sprat the other day, and she was ready to teach it to the boy until she found a book that said the lines were about Charles the First and his war with Spain."

Mary was on the stairs again, and she ran into the kitchen with a worn book held open to a reference. "Oh, no, you don't!" She waggled a finger under Nathanael's nose. "That harmless rhyme of yours was an attack on the friars for being more interested in food than faith."

"That's nonsense."

"It says so in black and white." She clapped the cover shut, raising a light dust. "What's more, I think you knew it. I know how you feel about ministers, Nat. Nothing would please you more than to see me filling my baby with that kind of poison."

"That's all," he said to himself. "Never again. Never."

"If you really want to do something constructive," Mary wheedled, "you get those books I asked you for."

"I can't. I cannot get at them. Won't you understand? They're locked up at the library. You have to be a famous scholar of about ninety years old to even get near them."

"I don't think that's fair. What about films? Don't all the fraternities show them?"

"You're really behind times." Often he flared at young Mary with more anger than their arguments deserved. "Nobody watches those movies any more. That was all right ten years ago for your pathetic friends. But we don't need that stuff."

Mary knew the reason for his temper. She kept her lips dry as she answered. "Those movies would be perfect for Laz right now. I remember some I saw from Japan, with everyone so courteous and smiling. And the men were not—you know —there was nothing about them to give him a complex later."

"I may be able to get some photographs," Nathanael relented. "A fellow I know drives over the border every weekend, and he could bring some back for me. I'd feel like a fool asking him."

"Explain," said Mary, "that you're protecting a little boy from bestiality."

When the argument over her theory of raising children had begun five years before, Nathanael had been a boy himself, and now he would have enjoyed debating with her. But Peter had ruled the subject closed.

The loudspeaker crackled and screeched once, and then a voice asked: "Have you seen Jesus? James is looking for him."

"No, Andrew," Martha called. "He left the grocery money on the table again early this morning. I haven't seen him."

Mary said, "Hello, James."

"What?"

"Mary said hello to James. That's all."

"This isn't a toy." Andrew's voice was muffled. "If she wants to talk with him, she can come upstairs."

"Never mind." Mary raised her voice. "I was only trying to be sociable."

"What?"

"For heaven's sakes, Andrew, fix your wires." Martha went back to frosting the cake.

"I have plans that will be even better," Andrew said slowly. His broadcasting voice was measured and calm, but he sounded excited. "I will tell you at dinner."

Left to herself in the kitchen, Martha finished icing the cake. She was shelling peas when old Mary threw open the one unboarded door and climbed inside.

"Mary," Martha said gently, "you know you're supposed to wait until dark. Someone might see you."

"This was important." The old woman glanced fitfully from side to side. "I ran out of pamphlets, and the plant will be letting out in forty-five minutes. I had to get more. They're the most popular messages I've ever had printed."

"Is this the one about the Devil controlling nine-tenths of the governments in the world?"

Mary nodded. "A lot of people didn't realize how bad things were going. They're so grateful to me for opening their eyes, they just can't do enough for me. One youngster got so mad he wanted to rush right out and start fighting wherever the Devil was strongest. I remember when my own flesh felt the same way."

"Are you selling this batch?" Martha wanted to distract her from a long faulting of Jesus.

"I'm giving them away. It's such an important message, I couldn't bear that it should go to just the people with money."

"How did you pay for the printing?"

Mary looked bland, her lying look. "I had a little money saved." Two mornings last week, there had been no grocery money left on the table, and Martha thought Jesus had forgotten. She would have to ask him to hide the bills and coins he left for her.

"Is Lazarus awake?" Old Mary liked to take the boy on her rounds and introduce him as her son.

"He's taking his nap." In dealing with his mother, Jesus countenanced any lie.

"I think I hear him upstairs. I'll run up and see."

"That's John. He's been pacing back and forth all afternoon. He's sure to have a poem to read to us at dinner."

"Do you know I asked him to write a few lines for me about the power of faith to rip the guts from the Devil's belly, and he wouldn't do it? What kind of a poet is he supposed to be?" Old Mary toyed with the wisp of hair she had allowed to fall over her forehead. "Do you understand one word of his poems?"

"I understand as much as he expects me to."

"Martha, listen to me." For her trade, old Mary had developed a slight hunch, together with a strident voice that carried over hecklers. At home her back straightened, but her voice was no less shrill.

"I can hear you."

"Come over here."

"We can't do that. Andrew's having trouble with his machine. If he can't record it, we'll have to repeat everything for him this evening."

"Martha!"

"Mary, you know I can't. Tell me whatever it is."

Old Mary's back was very straight now, and she held her shoulders imperiously. "I think I've got an offer."

"An offer? What kind of an offer?"

Mary gestured toward the door. "Oh, just an offer. Something that might let me broaden my scope and reach a lot more people."

"You don't mean you'd leave?"

Mary nodded vigorously as she said, "Oh, mercy, no!" She spoke directly into the loudspeaker. "Where could an old lady like me go? I'm just talking, Martha. Don't pay any attention to me."

Old Mary had left them before. Discussion of the details

was forbidden, but Martha knew the episode had pained Jesus. When she had been brought back, he had conferred with Andrew about fitting her with the same equipment they had developed for young Jimmy. In the end, they had decided against it.

Martha would have to report to Andrew the old lady's hint about a new departure. She disliked passing on that kind of information, and she hoped Andrew might draw his own conclusions from the pauses and weighting of Mary's words. But he wouldn't. Andrew, who had been a detective, heard everything that was said in the house. But it took James, who had been the chairman of a great charitable trust, to explain the meaning to him.

Old Mary had collected a stack of pamphlets from the drawer in the dining room buffet, and she was ready to ease open the outside door. "Good-bye, my dear," she called gaily to Martha. During the short walk to the gates of the computer plant, her head would begin to slump forward and the lines around her mouth would sag. Old Mary was convinced that joyousness attracted few converts, and she never smiled on the street corners.

"Hello, Aunt Martha. How are you today?" The child's greeting followed so closely on Mary's farewell that Martha expected the old woman to hear his voice and return to claim him. But the door stayed shut.

"Isn't it time for your nap already, Lazarus?"

"My mother says I have to go to bed early tonight so I don't have to take a nap."

Young Mary apparently expected a row at dinner over Andrew's proposal, whatever it might be. Lazarus, who had never heard a harsh word spoken, would be out of earshot on the third floor.

"Would you like a little prune juice?" The child knew their code and cried, "Oh, yes, please!" She cut a slab of chocolate cake for him, thinking that her deception was no better than the smirks and nods old Mary had used to cheat Andrew of an accurate transcript.

"This is good." He licked the rim of the frosting bowl. Someday soon, Martha thought, he will leave this house and sample other cakes and discover that I was a failure in the kitchen. Or does it happen the other way? Does he go through life believing that my cakes were perfect and every cake afterward is too moist, too rich, too filled with walnuts and fruit? If he does, he'll remember me fondly but he'll miss a hundred new flavors. How do you teach a child to pick out from the past only those things that fit him for the future? Raising a child is hard, Martha decided. But it is not a hardship I asked to be spared.

"I'm glad you liked it." She had never been reconciled to the boy's upbringing. Two years before, his mother had agreed that Martha could caution him about the stove in the apartment they were sharing. "All right," Mary had said, "but when you warn him, be sure to impress on him that the stove gets hot to cook his cereal in the mornings. He shouldn't think the stove likes burning him."

Martha had tried to use that opening to warn the child of other dangers. But he was very young, and Andrew was across town monitoring every word. "Remember, dear," she had said, "sometimes other things might seem as though they were going to hurt you, too."

The boy's blue eyes had filled with tears. "Is hurt like falling down, Auntie?"

"Sometimes. But you must remember that these things won't hurt you on purpose. Someone might make you feel bad without meaning to, and you should be ready to understand."

At that moment Andrew had interrupted. "Martha! You've told the boy what he needs to know. Don't you think he'd like to go out and play?" If the child had not been listening, Andrew's rebuke would have been blunter.

Afterward, she didn't try to warn Lazarus of the world outside his home. When Jimmy had first begun to watch the television set in the bedroom next to the boy's, she hoped Lazarus would overhear the sound of bullets and fists. But Andrew had covered Jimmy's walls and door with acoustical tile so that the sound from the set, the only one in the house, did not carry. Later the soundproofing had served a double purpose when Thaddaeus was bunked with Jimmy while he was taken off drugs. His groans would have kept everyone in the house awake.

"Before my nap, Uncle John let me look at the ocean for a long time," Lazarus said, and Martha thought, If we ever moved from the ocean, John's withdrawal pains would be as severe as Thad's were.

"I don't understand how you two can sit up there, cramped under the eaves, and watch the ocean all day long. It never changes, does it?"

"Uncle John says the ocean is never the same. He showed me how each wave is different until it comes in and licks the rocks on the shore."

"That's what they're doing, is it?"

"They get tired and swim back to the middle of the ocean, and they rest and come back. But when they come back, they're never the same."

"Why not?"

"Uncle John says licking the rocks changes them because licking is part of love, and after you've been in love you can't stay the same."

"Does all that make sense to you?"

"Yes." His nod was curt. "Doesn't it to you, Auntie?"

"Your Uncle John knows more about love than I do," she said. "He's devoting his life to research."

"My mother says when I grow up I'll know everything about love. She says everyone will come and want me to teach them because I'll know so much."

"Will you give lessons?"

"Wouldn't it be all right if I just touched them?"

"It might be better." She wondered if Mary saw the kind of Christ she was trying to raise—all laying on of hands and ignorant love.

"Where is Jesus?" The boy seemed prompted by her thoughts. "I never see him any more. Did Jesus go away?"

"He still sleeps in the room with you, but he gets up very early in the morning, and by the time he goes to bed you're already asleep."

"Why does he get up early?"

"To pray." Martha suspected that Jesus was addressing audiences again since he brought home a little money each night for stew meat and fresh oranges. But Jesus had pledged that he would not speak in public until he had heard once more the voice of God, and Martha was afraid to leave a note asking whether God had broken his silence. It was so much more likely that Jesus had broken his vow.

"I pray, too."

"Does God answer you?" Martha was sick of that question.

"He listens."

God listens the way Andrew does, she thought. As she was thinking of him, Andrew called, "James and I feel there must be something for the boy to do upstairs." Obedient, unquestioning, the boy heard the suggestion and ran out of the kitchen. With him gone, Martha could return to the peas.

But as she picked up a pod to crack, her world rang in her head and her eyes locked. Before she could bring them to focus again on her fingers, she felt that she had lived a lifetime.

Judas would have to explain someday why that happens. I'll force him to listen to me describe what comes over me and I'll ask, "Why do I see eternity in a pea pod, Judas?" Whatever he answers, I'll laugh once, sharply, and walk back to the kitchen. Then her sense of triumph evaporated, and she thought, He'll be able to explain it. He'll explain and explain, finally, everything I can think to ask him. And if I were cleverer and could make up better questions, he would answer those, too. Nathanael said it was the age, but it's only the stubbornness and pride of men without the grace to admit they don't know.

She wished again that Jesus had chosen a Judas who was an artist instead of the young man downstairs with his tubes and white rats. An artist might have painted a landscape on the boarded window over the sink or an enameled sunflower on the refrigerator door. Martha had no special taste for art, but she was not afraid of it, as she was sometimes afraid of the work under way in the basement.

When she had spoken to Peter about finding an artist, he had pointed out that they already had a poet and that Matthew, too, fancied himself artistic because of his book. That book had earned a considerable sum, which Matthew swore he had turned over to the government and the poor. In a paperbacked edition, it was still on display at the supermarket where Martha shopped, and she forced herself to tell Matthew whenever she had seen someone buying a copy.

"It may not be the greatest book in the world," Matthew liked to say, "but people seem to enjoy it. There's no harm in writing a simple, decent book that might do people a little good."

John hadn't answered him until Matthew, who had been a banker, once drew a comparison between his two occupations. "Writing isn't too much different from accounting," he had said. "You've got to be sure everything is clear and accurate so anyone looking at your books knows they're honest and balanced. If I have something to say, I say exactly what I mean. Life is too short for poetry."

"Life is too long without it," John answered. After that, he left the room whenever Matthew puffed on his pipe and talked about writing.

With the last pod cracked and the hard peas rattling like buckshot into the kettle, Martha could go to the living room for a few minutes of rest. It was the brightest room in the house, decked with lamps and strung with neon tubing. Any salvageable curtains and drapes from throughout the house had been hung in the living room, and they completely covered the boarded windows. The effect disturbed Martha. Where the boards could be seen in the other rooms, there was something inevitable about their confinement, as though the house itself had shut its eyes. In the living room the drapes seemed pulled against normal daylight, and the blame was transferred to the people who lived there. In her kitchen or bedroom Martha felt like a captive; in the living room, like a recluse; and she wondered which was more accurate.

The furniture that had escaped the fire was shabby and worn from twenty years of hard use. On the arms and back of the red plush chair, bristles had been rubbed away at the spots where hands and heads had rested. Touching the smoothness of those patches, Martha had decided that all the former tenants had been remarkably contrary. She pictured them as old men and self-indulgent women reclining deep in the chair, shaking their heads slowly as their answer to any request, any proposal. No, they said, oh, no, no. As they said no, their heads rolled back and forth, wearing down the bristles that tickled their necks.

These days Peter held their discussions around the table in the dining room. No one burst into the living room with a suggestion, and no one in the red chair had the chance to say no with a slow shake of the head. No one enjoyed the luxury of refusing from the depths of an overstuffed chair.

Sitting there, Martha tried to think of what life could still offer her that she would turn down. Romance? None of the men in the house saw her as a woman. Just as well, she told herself. With Jesus I may yet find something better than a man's love. What? He promised nothing. He warned that I was giving up the pleasures of life for a death that was empty and final. Do I believe that warning? Does Jesus believe it? Jesus, promising nothing, goes on promising everything to me. Each time I see his face, I see the promise I must believe.

They waited and their lives waited with them. Martha felt that in her twenty years with Jesus not a day had passed. But the years were passing when the days were not. She was nearly old. She could have been the mother of three of the men in the house and the grandmother of the boy. Unless— she thought with a fresh female feeling—Mary is older than twenty-five. Unless she lies about her age.

Was it a good life? Many nights Nathanael and Philip argued about that. She didn't read their transcripts any more. For her the question was settled. It was life. It was her life. She was used to it. When he had lived a few more years, Nathanael would start to feel comfortable with himself. He'd find that he could predict everything he would do or say. The mystery would be over. Martha believed in habit and Jesus, and they had never failed her at the same time.

A refrain ran through her head about the ingredients of little girls: "Sugar and spice and everything nice." Young Mary had refused to teach the rhyme to Lazarus because there had been another chorus about soldiers being made of drilling and killing. But the verse about little girls was true enough. Once Martha had been sugar and spice. Now she was saccharin—not caloric, not likely to raise the body's temperature. And she was salt, a seasoning without surprises. She frowned at the thought, and still she felt no regret. Saccharin was cheaper than sugar and healthier; she used it in most of her desserts. And salt was enough. Orégano and thyme were for young brides. As you got older, you simplified and you substituted. You learned that a couple of plain boxes on your shelf were worth all of the bright packets and tins and expensive containers. She was sure of that.

But against the worn upholstery she felt herself begin to shake her head.

Martha dozed for a moment under the lights. When they had first been required to prepare a summary of their dreams, she had learned to wipe away all traces as she awoke. Opening her eyes, she'd instantly forget the troubling shapes and voices. Last month young Mary had passed a note to her confessing that on many nights she dreamed of Jesus. Martha should have reported her. She did not, she told herself, from a sense of feminine loyalty.

Peter's heavy step woke her. He was a slender man who had trained in his youth until he could come down flat on the bottoms of his feet and sound, on the stairs, like a man twice his size. His pure light voice had been dragged down into his chest and made to rasp the way he thought a true soldier must speak. Wouldn't his troops have obeyed a musical sound, Martha wondered, or marched behind his graceful movements? Did a man have to be coarsened before he could command other men?

"Good evening, Peter."

"It is evening, isn't it? This room reminds me of a map room I once worked in. I seemed to be there only at midnight. When I see this much light, I assume there's a crisis somewhere in the world, and it's very late and I'm dead on my feet."

"Do you get tired, Peter?"

"I get tired. Martha, I have something to ask of you. First we'll get rid of the eavesdroppers." He strode to the speaker propped behind Martha's chair and spoke into it. "Turn this thing off."

"We can't do that." Andrew sounded aggrieved, but Martha knew he would already have one hand on the control button.

"Turn it off."

There was no way to tell that Andrew had obeyed, except
that the room became more still and the air did not seem to
be sucked in waves toward the speaker on the floor. Martha
knew it was her imagination; there was no way to tell.

"Thank you," Peter said into the speaker.

"He can't hear you."

"He'd better not be able to." Peter squatted on the floor
at her feet. He was trim enough to be able to fold down onto
the rug and not look like an old man's imitation of a young
one. Gazing down at him, Martha felt at a disadvantage—
too tall, too distant, her ankles and calves exposed but the
bottom of her face hidden by her breasts. Seated here above
him I should feel dominant, and I only feel clumsy.

"I'm going to speak frankly, Martha." Peter drew up his
knees and looked straight ahead. She wondered if he saw the
bruise on her leg. Her flesh discolored whenever the corner
of a table caught her thigh or Lazarus tugged too affectionately on her plump upper arms. She bruised like ripe fruit,
though she had begun to wither years ago.

"What is it?" It could not be that he would ask her to
leave. Peter didn't have that power. He couldn't drive her
away. Why did her heart start pounding?

"I'm worried about Jesus."

She felt her breath fall back into steady sighs. "Why?"

"When did you last see him?"

Martha had to think. In her imagination she saw him every
day while she cooked in the kitchen or dusted the dining
room furniture. "I can't remember. It may have been a
week."

"No one has talked with him for much longer than that.
He comes in late and goes out before anyone is awake."

"He leaves money for groceries. I find it on the table every
morning."

"How much?"

"Enough for meat and fruit and milk for the boy. We don't eat a lot in this house."

"Where does he get it?"

"I've never asked." She felt she could trust him with her apprehensions. "I think he may be speaking again and taking up a collection afterward."

"Begging." Peter's resignation sounded slightly contemptuous. "That's what I think. I think he's been begging for months."

"Why call it begging? It wasn't before." Martha thought, That's a question Nathanael should be asking. Young men are the ones who worry about definitions. Peter would tell him what he was now telling her: that when Jesus could offer salvation, he could stand before any audience and ask for money to advance his cause. Now Jesus had nothing to offer. And when you took money and gave nothing in return, that was begging. Peter was very definite. That was begging.

Nathanael and the other young men might care about Peter's definitions. Martha cared that Jesus came back each night, and she cared that there was money for food each morning on the kitchen table. What did young men have in their bellies that they could live on definitions and despise stew meat? Rapture, ideals and automobiles, that's what young men were made of.

"I'm sorry, Peter, I didn't hear you."

He was fussily annoyed. She could picture him thirty years ago, dressing down his platoon. Drilling and killing, that had been Peter's life before he became a ranking general. They forgot that too often. "I said the others have lost their faith."

"I don't understand you," Martha said. "We were promised nothing. He didn't ask us to believe. What faith could they lose?"

"You know better, Martha." His tone implied, You of all people. "The more often he told them they couldn't expect a reward, the closer they've huddled to await one. He knew how they'd react."

"Now you say they've lost a faith he didn't ask them for?"

"They go on living here, and they give Jesus perfunctory gestures of respect. But they don't believe anything. They don't even believe enough to move away. They don't believe enough to worry about not believing. They've settled in here, eating whatever's put before them, making do with boarded windows and two toilets, letting their words be written down. They've stopped connecting him with their reason for being here."

"We've never been very good at explaining why we followed him. Jesus hasn't minded that."

"Once he could explain for all of us. Now he can't."

"Peter," she said affectionately, "not all of us have as logical a mind as yours or James's. I know you want us to think straight, but some of us don't have the capacity. Isn't it enough that we're here? Isn't that enough for Jesus? It's enough for me."

"No, that's wrong." He was quiet but determined, and she decided to hear as little as she could and forget the rest. "Either we stay, hoping he will save us again, or we leave."

"Leave?" He was trying to get her out after all. What difference to her if he forced out everyone else with her? But he had no power. They could resist him. They were not his squad, and they could tell him no. Or better still, ignore him.

He said, "We didn't come here for an easy life. We came to be with Jesus. And he can't be with us because he's out begging for our daily bread."

"We don't know he's begging."

Peter looked up from the seam in her stocking. "That's true," he said. "He might be stealing."

She let him see that she was shocked and hurt. "I understand now why you made Andrew turn off the speaker. You can't be very proud of what you're saying."

"You're young enough to be my daughter, Martha, even if you look like an old woman, all hunched there in your black dress. I'm talking to you because I worry about you—about all of them, but especially about you."

"I'll think about what you've said." She rose and stepped over his feet to reach the speaker in the dining room. "We've finished," she called into it. "Andrew, do you hear me?"

"I hear."

"You can turn on the machine in the living room again."

"Can you give me a summary of what you said? I'll need something for the transcript."

"We talked about money."

"Is there a problem?" Andrew sounded alarmed.

"Not at all. Peter and I were discussing the food budget. It was too dull for you to bother with."

"All right." He didn't believe her, but no one in the house lied, except to old Mary. "With the troubles I've had up here today, one more break in the tape won't matter."

"Thank you."

"Isn't it time for dinner?"

"I'm going out now to start the vegetables."

"Thaddaeus is in the kitchen."

"He can help me."

She was glad to have the warning. The boy annoyed her, and she needed a chance to hide her feelings. "Hello," she greeted him. "You're in time to help set the table."

He's handsome, she thought with the amazement she felt each time she had to look at him. Until he answers, he's handsome.

"I can't move, hardly," Thaddaeus said, twisting his fine features to scowl at her. "I keep getting these pains in my back. It hurts even when I lie in bed."

When he gave up drugs, he had begun to complain of two dozen aches and ailments. To Martha, he had been much easier to bear when he punctured his arm twice a day in the upstairs closet and collapsed on his bed. Peter and the others had decided that his existence was living death, and he'd been locked into the tiled room until his need was gone. Now what were these endless complaints of his? If not living death, then living sickness, living disease. Martha pushed aside her feeling that they should have left Thaddaeus alone. The majority had decided he was better now, and she believed that the majority was never wrong. Her only strength had come at times that she belonged to the majority.

"I've got some wine stuck away in the cupboard." She tried to sound so competent the wine would cure him in spite of himself. "It will float away some of those aches."

"Nothing helps." With a fingernail, he was digging deep lines into the oilcloth on the kitchen table. Stop that! she wanted to scream at him. Cut your nails and clean them! For once, don't whine when you talk to me! For once! No whining!

She took the oilcloth from under his hand and rolled methodically, as though it were a task she performed every night. I can't even bring myself to snatch it away from him. I like to pretend I'd have let him shoot poison in his arm because I'm indifferent to his misery. But it's because I'm too soft to make anyone stop anything. I'd rather spare his feelings than his life.

"Try it anyway. One glass won't make an alcoholic out of you."

"They'd like that," he said bitterly.

"Who'd like what?"

"The others. They'd like it if I was a drunk."

Martha ignored the recorder. Today's transcript would be long, and only Andrew would read it all. "Maybe we would like it, Thad. Without some weakness, you don't seem to be much of anything. At least we'd know who you were."

"Like Thad the Junkie?"

"That's right. We'd recognize you again. Some people seem

to need more than a name. They need something hooked on like a label."

"Thad the Wino." He turned it over on his tongue. "Thad the Drunk."

"Wine would have several advantages. It's cheaper than what you were using, and it's easier to get."

"Drinking still wouldn't help my back any."

"Perhaps not." She saw she'd have to give him some reassurance. "No, it certainly wouldn't cure you completely. But your pains would give you a reason to drink until you didn't need reasons any longer."

"Are you kidding me?"

"I don't think so." She took from the cupboard their unmatched dishes—bone china, pink plastic, pottery with lilies of the valley glazed around the rims. "My own shortcoming could be attached to my name, too. Martha the Cook."

He drummed his dirty nails on her breadboard. "I'd probably feel better if the food around here wasn't so bad. I'm probably not getting enough vitamins."

"You don't eat the food. You only eat bread and mashed potatoes."

"Why don't we get somebody who can cook?" She ignored him. "Why don't we get a man or somebody who knows something about cooking?"

"Why don't you learn and teach me?" Thad the Teacher. Thad the Chef.

"I can't be standing around with my hands in water and all that. The pain already shoots from my shoulder down to my elbow. Most mornings I can't even move my arms. I need more sunlight. It's too dark in here. It's not healthy."

"You look better than you did."

"I don't feel better. You don't know what it was like." She had heard that theme before. Whatever he said, she remained convinced that any vision granted to Thaddaeus could only be of pimples and dog dirt. "You lie back," he was saying, "and you're on top of everything, and there's beautiful colors—"

I can't help it: We should have left him alone. We have nothing better for him. We should have left him his white dust. John says I am an elitist and that's why I side so often with James and Andrew. That's not true. I am practical. We practical people form our own elite.

She said, "Put these plates on the table and push the dinner buzzer, will you please?"

He grabbed up the plates and shuffled off. I will not eat from that green delft plate on top, not after seeing his filthy hands clamped all over it. I'll slip it over to Matthew, who is too pure to be infected. But he'll see it is one of our better plates, and he'll say, "Why the special treatment? Did my royalty check come today?" And he'll laugh so we know he's impersonating a boor to amuse us. John won't laugh, and later Matthew will say, "I should know better by now than to mention royalties in front of our poet, even in jest."

I'll give the delft to old Mary.

She turned on the gas under the kettle of peas. She turned it off. I should remember what mush they make if I start them now. I do this every day. Why doesn't it get easier for me?

While she was at the stove, she pulled open the oven door to look at the turkey. No one else knew they weren't having hash tonight or scrambled eggs. The butcher had kept cutting the price on an unsold turkey until she could afford it. Why wasn't one of them a butcher?

The turkey had begun to brown, and Martha ladled a little juice over its meaty breast. Too bad, she thought, that my own body will never be that appetizing to someone. Too bad we don't eat our dead. It might be a comfort for the bereaved if they could get out knives and forks after the funeral and baste their mothers or their sons. Who'd eat me? The state would serve me to hungry men in Simon's charity kitchens.

She shuddered. Jesus would like that. Jesus would like to lie across the table each night and urge us to eat our fill. He sees something I can't see. I'm left with a picture of rib bones and ear lobes pushed to the side of the plate. She let the oven door slam shut.

What next? The potatoes had to be mashed. She took from the cupboard a heavy yellow bowl and a wire masher like the one they had used in her home when she was a girl. Peter apologized occasionally for not being able to buy modern utensils, but she enjoyed gripping the crockery bowl between her legs and bludgeoning each potato into paste. Again she was a little girl, but stronger and unsupervised, and she sought out the lumps, not to avoid a scolding, but because she wanted no lumps in potatoes she had prepared. She was pleasing herself; and she was doing exactly what the little girl had been told to do thirty years ago.

When the potatoes were whipped, she washed a head of lettuce and cut up six tomatoes for the salad. She tossed them together in a bowl, inspected the result and tossed a second time. She had not produced a salad. She was left with chunks of lettuce and pulpy tomato. The others were accustomed to the food she brought to the table, and they might see a salad in the bowl.

The buzzer had brought them downstairs. Martha heard them talking quietly as they took their usual places around the table. "Hello, sweetheart!" Judas was up from the basement, hanging his white jacket on a nail over the staircase. "Ah, sweet mystery of life," he sang, as he sang every night.

"Did you have a good day?"

"Yes! Yes!" Judas was bouncing with enthusiasm. "You're going to be proud of me, beautiful. I'm curing your woes."

"All I ask is that you don't let the rats get out again."

"I never did find Dinah." He rolled his brown eyes under their long lashes. "That reminds me, just what are we having for dinner tonight?"

"That's disgusting."

"No, that was last night. Tonight's Friday—it should be repulsive."

Martha opened the oven door. "Dinah!" he cried. "How could you roast my most successful experiment?"

"Never mind," she said. "Don't go in there and ruin everybody's appetite with talk about rats."

"You're a good lady, Martha." He kissed her cheek wetly. "I'm proud of you, anyway."

"You wouldn't say that if we were having eggs." After four years of experimenting with different kinds of eggs, Judas couldn't face them at dinner. When Martha served scrambled eggs, he shared pork liver with old Mary's cat.

Judas pointed to the oven. "Isn't that your notorious omelet in there? It's dark and swollen enough."

"If you had company down in the basement, you wouldn't be so foolish at night."

"Andrew was talking to me most of the afternoon over the speaker. He wanted some advice on his plan. Have you heard about it?"

"He said he'd explain tonight."

"It's very ingenious. Andrew is no scientist, but he knows what he's doing." She laughed sharply, and he kissed her again. "I'll win you over. I'll do for you what I did for Dinah."

"Kept her caged, shot her full of needles and then lost her?"

"She's immortal."

"Someday we'll all be immortal."

"Do you believe that, Martha?"

His earnestness surprised her. "I think so," she said, ducking her cheek away from his puckered lips. "No more kissing. Say something nice at the table about the turkey."

"I hate to take an unpopular stand."

"You were never known for your courage."

"I eat my share," he said cheerfully.

"Judas—" she had been thinking about his question—"to believe something is going to happen isn't the same as wanting it to happen."

"Isn't it?"

"I know it's fashionable now to think the two are the same, but they're not."

"You're not asking me to stop my work?"

"I don't want you to think I approve," Martha said.

"Do you disapprove?"

"Leave me alone," she said, vexed with herself. "I have a dinner to put on the table."

"Have you a message to convey to the assembly?" He pointed through the kitchen door.

"Take in the bread, please. That's all."

"There's only your menacing rye on this plate. Where's your treacherous homemade white?"

"I stuffed the turkey with it."

"Double jeopardy."

"The bread."

He saluted and kicked open the swinging door. Everyone seemed to be in his place. A chair for Jesus stood empty at the head of the table. "Hurry up, Martha," Andrew called. "I want to make my presentation while we're on our soup."

The soup! Martha let the door swing closed and hurried to light the gas under last night's bean soup. The caldron would take too long to heat. She poured the thin brown soup into three smaller sauce pans and put one over each burner. The peas she moved to her breadboard.

By the time she had found her ladle and filled the tureen with hot soup, Martha could hear loud voices from the next room. She put her shoulder lightly to the door, to be sure it wasn't blocked, then pushed harder on it and emerged backward into the dining room.

"It's unnecessary," John was saying, and young Mary was

talking over him. "Oh, Ecce, everyone knows why you'd be opposed."

"As things are now, we're missing a lot," Andrew said. "Isn't that right, James?"

Martha leaned against the wall to hear James's comments. He could make things clear to her, a talent for which she couldn't always thank him.

"We all know," James began, "that not everything that goes on in this house is recorded in the transcript. We have found notes, for one thing, proving that efforts have been made to circumvent our procedures. The writers of those notes have apologized, and I raise the matter now only to demonstrate that our present system is not completely effective."

"A few notes," John said deprecatingly.

"I'd agree with you that they are not in themselves serious."

"Then what's the—?" Thaddaeus had every right to speak but no guarantee the others would listen. He broke off.

"I think we would all agree," James continued, "that we live together under considerable difficulty with a minimum of stress. Is there any dissent to that evaluation?"

Around the table everyone looked at his plate or shook his head. Old Mary said, "No trouble, no trouble."

"Anyone thinking about the matter objectively must recognize," James said, "that we have been able to avoid trouble largely because of our agreement. No one need worry that others in the house are plotting against him, ridiculing him or laying plans in which he could not participate. At any moment, the day's full transcript of conversation—most of it tedious beyond belief—is available to him. He need harbor no suspicions and build no defenses. The total lack of privacy, at first so repugnant to some of you, has furnished us with complete peace of mind."

"We've become omniscient," Matthew said jovially.

"About what is said." John rose to Matthew's lure. "Not about what is thought."

"I'll amend my statement for the benefit of our purist," Matthew smiled tolerantly. "Because of the loudspeakers we know everything that's worth knowing."

Using the tip of his spoon, John drew a string of pork from the soup and laid it like a fly on the saucer beneath his bowl.

"Ecce—" young Mary seldom spoke at conferences unless her dislike of John had been awakened—"you have to admit that there's been no restriction here. There's only the need to keep a record. If Andrew wants to install closed-circuit screens—"

Is that what he wants? Martha thought. After all, why not? She did nothing she'd be ashamed to do in front of a camera. Why did she feel herself wanting to object?

"Some of you are experiencing the same kind of emotional distaste you felt years ago when we first asked you to record your conversations," James said. "At that time Peter pointed out that your objections were falsely based and your feelings illogical. Perhaps, Peter, you could review your explanation for those who have forgotten or were too young to appreciate its justice."

"Certainly." Peter would be at his best, using a butter knife as a pointer. "I said at that time, and Jesus agreed with me, that many of us who had fallen into doubt about the existence of God were nonetheless basing our entire ethical system on traditional religious morality."

"What do you mean?" College had taught Nathanael that calling out a question could carry him through those classes for which he was not prepared.

"If you don't interrupt," said Peter, who had taught only at a military academy, "you'll find that everything will be clear when I've finished."

"Sorry."

"Many of us still assume, despite all evidence to the contrary, that man has inherent dignity and honor, that he was, in fact, created in God's image. One of the hardest lessons for me to learn—as painful as it was crucial—was that men require endless discipline and supervision."

"Army men do." John was sifting through his soup for more pork. His head bowed, he sounded deferential.

"All men." Peter's tone was as flat as John's had been. "When at last I accepted the full consequences of my disbelief in God, then all the hidden microphones and long-range spying devices became inevitable."

Andrew said, "It's not as though we used them for—"

"You're quite right." Peter liked his interruption no better than Nathanael's. "Along with our new techniques for observation and, when necessary, control, has come a tolerance for man's weaknesses that we did not enjoy during more spiritual times."

"As our poet has every reason to know." James should not join in the assault on John, Martha thought. Their deviations might not be as striking as his, but they all expected sympathy for something.

"No one has ever prevented me from doing as I wished," John said dryly. "That doesn't mean I want a camera trained on my bed."

"Why not?" several of them asked.

"It offends me."

"Why?" James pursued the question.

John put aside his spoon. "I can't give you a logical answer, and you won't accept anything else. I could talk about privacy, delicacy, taste, sensitivity, and you'd prove to me logically that I sacrificed all claims to those qualities when I gave up God."

"I think we could prove that." James was sober, not smug.

"I'll spare you the trouble. I'll admit I'm suffering from a kind of hangover. I've swallowed too much talk about the soul."

"Some practical training would have helped to—"

"Matthew, I'm not finished." Peter spoke directly to John. "I'm not saying that because we accept your odd tastes you are obliged to follow our wishes. That's the first argument that comes to my mind, but I reject it for the same reasons you do. What I'm asking is that you consider the reasons for Andrew's request and determine honestly whether the sacrifices we have asked in the past have hindered you personally more than they have benefited all of us as a group."

"It's a question of priorities—" James began, and Martha returned to the kitchen. They would win John over. He'd spend more time at the attic window and more time on the beach at midnight, looking for a body to fondle. But he'd stay with them. Poetry had not made him strong, only dissatisfied. Martha moved the peas to the top of the stove and bent down for the turkey. The bird was crisp and brown across the breast. She cut the strings that had held in her bread-crumb dressing. When Peter finished carving, she'd ask him to put aside several large slices of white meat for Jesus. Was everyone else there? No. Martha had seen an empty chair near the sideboard. Who sat between Nathanael and Simon?

She hurried back to the dining room and leaned over Andrew's shoulder. James was still talking, and everyone was intent on his quiet argument.

"Andrew—"

"In a minute, Martha. I want to hear this."

"Where's Jim?"

He glanced across the table and began searching his pockets until he produced a metal cartridge with five small bulbs, all of them dark. "My battery is dead," he said to the room at large. "James, Peter, will you come with me? Thomas, you'd better come, too. I've lost contact with Jim."

As he spoke, a low noise sounded overhead, and all the men ran for the stairs. The two Marys followed. It's nothing, Martha assured herself. Nothing has happened. Jimmy will turn up in a minute. Lazarus has suffered nothing more than a bad dream.

With a grunt she lifted the turkey from the oven, transferred it to their meat platter and carried the large bird into the dining room. She had not put down her burden when Andrew appeared, holding the child's limp body. Martha dropped the turkey to the sideboard and cleared a spot in the center of the table, under the chandelier. "Lay him here."

Behind Andrew, Jimmy came in with the rest of the men. "Hello, Aunt Martha," he said pleasantly.

"What have you done, Jim?"

"I think I've killed Lazarus, ma'am." He scratched at the long blond hair that covered five shaved spots on his skull.

"Why, Jim?" Martha spoke to him across Lazarus' body. Peter was probing under the child's eyelids, and Philip had his ear to the small chest.

"I don't know, ma'am."

"He nearly broke the child's neck," Matthew said. "Do you see those marks?"

"Why didn't Laz try to get away?" His mother had begun to weep. "Why didn't he scream?"

"There's no heartbeat at all," Philip said. "He's dead."

The others stared down at the dead boy or searched the face of his killer. Martha was the only one in the room to look at Judas. He saw her look and shook his head. Young Mary's sobs were louder, and old Mary was chanting prayers. In the confusion, Martha looked at Judas again.

He scowled and seemed angry, but he slipped away to the basement, and Martha knew he had agreed. She raised the boy to undo the buttons on his pajamas. No one stopped her. They think women know instinctively what to do, she thought. They assume I am performing some rite. As she pulled off the striped cotton bottoms, the boy's skin was warm in her hands and his legs bent easily.

When the body was naked in her arms, she laid it back on

the table and draped it with a corner of the white tablecloth. Keeping her hands busy, she dipped a napkin in a water glass and lightly wiped the boy's face. Her scrubbing made his lips move like rubber under the cloth.

By the time Judas returned, she had washed both arms, colder now, from the elbow to the shoulder. She didn't know which side Judas would prefer for the injection.

"Do you want to be alone?" she asked.

"I don't care."

None of them, including Peter, who had authorized the experiments years ago, seemed to understand what Judas was about to try. I'm the only one with faith, Martha thought. I believe in everyone.

"Press his eyelids shut, will you?" Judas turned to her, and she became his nurse at the operating table. The others had stopped existing for her. There were Judas and the corpse and Martha the Nurse.

She did as he asked. "Why?"

"Dinah used to be blind for twenty minutes or so when I did the experiments under strong lights. I finally blindfolded her and plugged her ears." He spoke easily, and he was not foolish.

"Should I get cotton for his ears?"

Judas laughed and gestured around the table. "Do you hear a sound in this room?"

"Do you want hot water?" Martha asked.

"No, I'm going to be a lot less messy than nature is."

"Is there anything you do need?"

"You mean, why don't I begin?" Judas smiled at her. "I'm afraid, Martha, that's why. When my own pulse slows down, I'll see about getting his going."

They waited. Judas chuckled to himself several times, but Martha, his assistant, found she wasn't annoyed by his nervous humor. After two or three minutes had passed, he asked, "Shall we start? Hand me that hypodermic, will you?" Martha gave it to him. She had never seen the needle Thaddaeus had used. Presumably it had been no different from this one.

Judas inserted the tip into a vial of amber liquid and filled the needle's small glass tank. He was about to push the point into the boy's arm when old Mary said, "Let us pray."

"Shut up!" Martha's voice surprised her. She had never said that before to anyone.

The room was quiet when Judas pricked the dead skin. The fluid ran through his needle into the body. Nothing happened. "It will take a few minutes." Judas sounded apologetic. "The reaction takes a little while."

They waited. Martha saw the boy's left eyelid quiver. It's my own eye blinking, she told herself. But John had seen something, and he turned his head away. Philip asked, "Is it working?" Judas didn't answer.

Young Mary lurched toward the table, but Peter held her back or held her up. He kept his fingers around her elbows. "It won't work," old Mary said.

"It will." Thomas spoke gently to her.

Martha thought, If the boy's arm moved then, as it seemed to, the movement was rigor mortis, death tightening its grasp. Boys and men don't have a second chance to live. Women come to life again when they give birth. That can't be a miracle because it happens every second. Once Jesus could have brought the boy back to life, and tonight he's not even here. Judas is not Jesus. Judas is nothing but a man. Only women and gods can give life. Fertile women and potent gods. Judas is a man, and I am not even a mother. Neither of us knows the secret of life.

Something made a noise. Simon the social worker had coughed at the same time, and no one could be sure that the boy had moaned. Then he moaned again, and young Mary fell back against Peter's chest.

Martha thought to look at Jimmy. His lips worked with pain. Judas had destroyed his handiwork and his name. What will he be if he can't be Jim the Killer, Jim the Threat?

Judas held a cupped hand over the child's eyes and talked to him in a monotonous voice. "Don't move for a minute, son. Lie there and breathe slowly. Nothing is going to happen. Your mother is here. Lie still and let the breath come out of your mouth. Everything is all right. Everything is fine."

The boy was whimpering. "He hurt me. He hurt me."

Ask why. Martha felt herself growing angry. Ask this roomful of experts why he killed you. Ask them and force even Judas to say, "I don't know."

"It's all right, Laz," his mother crooned. "It was an accident. No one wanted to hurt you."

"He hurt my neck." The boy's eyes were open but glazed. The strong light seemed to daze him.

"We'll talk about it later, sonny," Peter said. "Now you'd better go upstairs to bed."

"I don't want to go up there," Lazarus sobbed. "He'll hurt me again. I don't want to, Mama."

"Don't be afraid," young Mary said and stopped. The boy didn't know the word. "Mama will take you to your room and sit by your chair. No one is going to hurt you."

With twitching in his arms and legs, the child raised himself on the table, and Judas lowered him to the floor. Hesitantly he let his mother take his hand and draw him to the stairs.

"Good night, Lazarus. Pleasant dreams." Judas was subdued, almost solemn. Why isn't he celebrating? Martha wondered. He should rush around the room and shake hands and whoop with excitement.

"Congratulations," Peter said when the boy had gone. "I didn't think it was possible."

"I wasn't sure myself. The one rat that responded to the formula has disappeared. I don't know how long she lived afterward. The boy may be dead in the morning."

"But you could revive him again?"

"I suppose so. I have a lot more work to do before I can

make any claims at all. It has seemed to work twice. That's as much as I can say."

The others had taken their places around the table. Martha left the turkey on the sideboard. Her own stomach was uneasy, her heart was racing; she assumed everyone felt the same. Jimmy was probably the only one who could eat. He'd take each helping with a word of thanks and eat with unfailing good manners. She caught his eye across the table, and he smiled at her, boyishly, charmingly.

If we were being painted tonight, she thought, everyone who saw the picture would wonder whether that golden head belonged to Jesus. Or am I wrong? If the artist was good enough, could he make them see that the candid eyes fall a fraction short of focusing? Could he catch the slight break in the molding of the mouth? No, even my eye seldom sees the small flaws in Jimmy's beauty. The painting would either show an angel or a monster, and that's why I have never let myself believe in art.

When she listened again, young Mary had come back to the table and Peter was speaking. Something he had said caused the others to protest. "I don't understand that conclusion," Matthew was saying, and Nathanael, close to tears, kept repeating, "It doesn't seem right."

James gave no sign that he was agitated, but he cut in above the others. "Let us at least wait until Jesus comes back and we can discuss it with him."

"No," Peter said firmly. "For the reasons I gave, there is no decision to be made. We must leave."

How has he managed to twist what Judas accomplished into an argument for doing what he has wanted to do for months? Martha tried to listen more carefully. Excitement scrambled her thoughts, and even when she heard she was not sure she was understanding.

"Judas has eliminated death." Peter sounded as though he were speaking to a group of children.

"It looks as if, within the foreseeable future, death can be forestalled indefinitely," Judas said.

"Judas has eliminated death," Peter repeated in exactly the same way. "With death gone, we have no need for a God, and we have no need for Jesus."

The others began to protest again. "God will punish you," old Mary cried.

"What will he do?" Peter asked. "Strike me dead?"

"Whatever the outcome of all this—" Matthew drew deep on his pipe stem—"Jesus and his teachings will continue to be a useful moral guide for life on earth."

"I think when you've had time to consider, Matthew, you'll change your mind." Peter looked young and exhilarated as he leaned across the table on his knuckles. "Every value in our world is based on death, particularly those values Jesus brought us. Let Andrew tell us, What will a policeman do when there is no death?"

Andrew was not a stupid man, but he thought slowly and again they had to wait. "There'd be no murder," he said at last. "The victim could be revived with an injection."

"And no war," Nathanael volunteered.

"And no war," Andrew repeated. "I wouldn't think people would steal. At least all the things I've ever wanted to own wouldn't have seemed important if I'd known I was never going to die."

He stopped, and after a minute or two it was clear he had finished. Peter said, "Tell us about poetry, John."

"I wouldn't even try." Whenever John spoke at the table, his voice was deep. "Of course Peter is right. Everything I do is done to keep death at arm's length. Death dictated the lines I've written, and death has driven me out on the beach to find comrades to fight death at my side."

"Death is God," Philip said ironically.

"Yes," John agreed, "and now Judas is giving us what we had always thought we wanted, life everlasting."

"Eden without an exit," said Nathanael, encouraged by the smile that had greeted Philip.

John ignored him. "If anyone had asked me this morning whether I'd care to live without poetry, I'd have said no. To-night, when I ask myself whether I'd ever write throughout an eternal lifetime, I have to say that I would not."

"Why not, if you're so dedicated?"

"Because, Matthew, the need would be gone. Even you would find after the first three hundred years or so that you'd forgotten the combination to your secret strongbox."

"That's—"

"If you had one," John amended, and Matthew closed his mouth on his protest.

To young Mary, Peter said, "Tell us about love."

Her mouth had turned into a rueful curve, almost like John's. "I'll tell you what I remember," Mary said. "I was eighteen when I met Lazarus' father, and my body sprang open like a trap. My mind's mouth opened, and I began to chew him with teeth I didn't know I had. I wanted to feed on him and suck the life out of his body. But I wanted his teeth sharper than mine so that as I devoured him he destroyed me."

"Not love," old Mary said. "Satan's lust."

"Then it ended."

"Why?" John asked.

She forgot her antagonism and spoke to him. "Because I wanted more than the most he could give me. I poked around until I found a small hidden part of him that he couldn't give up, and then I tormented him for that part until he ran away from me."

"Why did you do it?"

"I never knew why. I guess I wanted to discover the secret of life, and I was willing to rip open my lover's heart to find it."

"And all that time," Philip said, "it was in a test tube in the basement."

"And now?" Peter asked her.

"I don't like to say it, but I think I could take him for his body and his heart and leave him whole."

"Is that love?" John asked her.

"It's not what I had before. I think it may be sweeter."

"What if he left again?"

"If he left again, John, I'd have eternity to find another lover. I wouldn't be waking up with my life half gone and a new fold of fat around my hips. I wouldn't be wondering if I'd get lucky before my breasts started to fall. If Judas let me live forever at this age, I could manage without love."

"Not without the love of God," old Mary said. "You think you're scientific and modern, but you can't get along without God."

Matthew said, "God had one salable item, and Judas has copied it and offered it at a cheaper price. God has been underbid, Mary. God isn't competitive any more."

"It seems to me," Martha said, "that if we must give up love and beauty, Judas has set his price too high."

Peter answered sharply, "Judas doesn't ask anything. If John finds he can't write more joyful hymns to life without death hanging over his head, that's hardly Judas' fault. John could refuse the treatment."

"Could I?"

"What do you propose, Peter?" James asked.

"Let me ask you first, What happens to Jesus when there is no death? Who will speak for him?"

"Let me," Thomas said. "I'll be Jesus for a minute and tell you what he'd say."

"He's weak," old Mary said, and they knew she didn't mean Thomas. "I can't believe he's my son."

"Hush. Go ahead, Thomas."

"I am Jesus then." Thomas hooked his thumbs into his belt, and his crisp white shirt bulged out below his vest. "Except for what Judas did tonight, I could have gone on forever trying to recapture the faith I had lost. I'd be born again, rage against God's silence and die. And in the hearts of a few men, my anguish would continue to ignite small fires. Even when doubts overcame me, I could go on because there was no question more important. Tonight Judas has made no question less important."

"What will you do?" Peter asked.

"What I have always done: I'll go on trying to reach God. There is nothing else for me. John is a man and he can stop writing poems. Mary is a woman and she can stop looking for love. I am nothing but the search for God. When the search ends, I die."

"How can you keep on?"

"I am shrewd, you know. It's a side of me you have never cared to recognize. But I am shrewd, and I know you better than you admit. On a spring morning I'll try to persuade John to write a verse. For young Mary, I'll celebrate love—sheer, earthly love—with lyricism you've never heard. I'll do all of that to keep my search alive within you.

"But I will be trying to lure you to pleasures you no longer need and to visions you don't want to dream again. I'll be a serpent tempting you with love and art and the beauty of pain. You'll shun me first and then you'll despise me, for Nathanael told you right. There will be no escape from the Eden to which Judas is leading you."

One of the men said, "We should let Jesus talk for himself."

"No." Peter had risen again to his feet. "Thomas told the truth."

James said, "One thing we haven't considered is the effect on the population when they hear of this discovery. Not only will there be panic among the fatally ill, but every mother will turn up at Judas' laboratory with her children."

"I'm trying to make you understand that the full results are still a long way off."

"We understand, Judas," Peter said. "Where could you advance your techniques more quickly?"

"Any large laboratory. A private university would be nicest, I suppose."

"With government money?"

"I don't care."

Peter turned to James, who was polishing his rimless glasses on cloth he carried for that purpose. "You can arrange that, can't you?"

"If I return to the foundation, the staff can locate a congenial campus and obtain all of the funding he requires."

"Andrew and I will go back to the capital," Peter said. "I foresee even greater need during the next few years for widespread adoption of Andrew's methods. I will re-establish myself so that when a selection committee is formed, my chairmanship will be assured."

"Do you mean some people will get the treatment while others are allowed to die?" young Mary asked.

Peter nodded. "It's all the more important that the selection be made intelligently. You perhaps have ideas, Judas, about whom should be given priority?"

"I don't care." He smiled vaguely. "Do you think," he asked James, "that you can find a place with a lot of windows? It's been spooky down in that basement."

"You can discuss those details tonight on the plane," Peter said.

Several excited voices asked, "Plane?"

"I think it's vital that we start immediately. If I make the necessary calls tonight, the appropriate officials can be waiting for you in the capital and at the foundation headquarters."

Peter's movements were brisk and his cool gray eyes glowed. "Nathanael, Thaddaeus and young Jim will come with me. Andrew, is his wiring working again?"

"It was the battery on my control unit." Andrew was lugubrious. "It wasn't Jim's fault. I'll work out a monitor with spare batteries so it can't happen again."

"Fine. I think Simon should go with you, James. His experience among the poor might prove helpful. The foundation had better be preparing a guideline for the selection process that our committee can adopt when the time comes. Matthew, that might appeal to you."

"It would be an opportunity for me to combine my concern for people with whatever small writing talents I may possess."

"Good. Philip, you understand the need for secrecy, of course?"

The reporter's round face had sunk into seriousness. "I believe this is clearly one of those occasions when the public interest requires discretion. I thought if I sat in with this committee you're forming, I'd be prepared to present the information in the most thorough and factual manner when the time comes."

"That seems satisfactory." Peter surveyed the room. "The ladies—for observation, Lazarus will have to live near Judas. Will a campus suit you, Mary?"

"I guess."

"You don't have to worry about me," old Mary said. "Not that anyone would. You're so wrapped up in this so-called science that you don't even see God's miracle when it hits you in the face."

Peter waved down Judas' protest. "If Mary wants to identify as God that process by which you learned to understand acids and enzymes, we have no reason to object."

"God walked right into this room," old Mary said. "He heard my prayers, and he brought the innocent child back to life. I've been making plans for getting the gospel out to more people, and now I'll really have something to tell them."

"Peter!" Philip cried. "She'll tell everybody."

"The way she'll tell it, it won't matter," Thomas said, and as he spoke, Peter remembered him. "Where will you go, Thomas?"

"All of a sudden, I want to sail around the world." The usual mocking look was gone from his face. "I hadn't realized the hold he had on me."

"Martha?" Peter was ready to adjourn. "You'd better go with Judas and young Mary."

"I don't think so." The younger men were moving their chairs away from the table, and her answer went unheard.

As he rose, James said, "I'll get working on a laboratory for Judas."

Andrew was already on the stairs. "Peter, you can use the telespeaker in my control room to make plane reservations."

Peter was assigning chores. "Nathanael, you help Judas crate his equipment. Try to keep the boxes to a minimum. Anything he can buy later, leave behind. Within a week we'll have ample money available to us."

Matthew said, "Actually I came upon some royalty checks this morning that I'd completely overlooked. If you're sure I'll be reimbursed, I could turn them over to you instead of sending them to my customary charities."

Peter followed Matthew to his room. Over his shoulder, he called, "Thaddaeus, Jim, help the women pack."

Martha had picked up the turkey, but Jimmy eased it away from her and carried the platter into the kitchen. "May I help you pack, ma'am?" He turned his friendly smile on her at its full force. "You're my favorite lady in this house, I guess you know that. I'd like to help you any way I could."

"Old Mary seemed eager to be on her way." Martha could not look at him. "I wish you'd help her instead."

"Whatever you say. I'm sorry we didn't have time for the turkey. I guess it was sort of my fault."

"Andrew said it wasn't."

When he swung open the door to leave her, Martha heard sounds and voices all over the house. Drawers slammed open and shut, quick steps echoed on the stairs, light switches clicked on and water was running in two washbowls. They were leaving, and they were happy. Peter had won. Or Judas. Or Jim.

John found her at the sink washing soup bowls. "I heard what you told them."

"You didn't say anything about your plans."

"No one asked."

"Where are you going, John?"

"Down to the ocean."

"After that?"

He raised his eyebrows. She saw that he was carrying a book. "Isn't that the boy's Testament?"

"They weren't packing it. I used to hate this copy because his mother had torn out the crucifixion. Tonight it seemed like the version to have."

Martha thought, If I said the one right word, I might save his life. But if I argue at all, I might go to the ocean with him. He wouldn't have to say a thing. I'd talk myself into the water. "Is there anything I can say?"

He shook his head. "Just promise that you'll leave tonight with the others. If you wait, you'll hurt Jesus more than he deserves."

"I'll try."

"Look at me. As long as you stay, Jesus will stay with you. Don't do that to him. He's dead. Don't make him walk any more. Let him lie down. Let him be quiet."

He had convinced her. She could leave a note where Jesus put the money each night. What could she say? She could thank him. For the money.

"Good-bye."

"Good night, John."

He went out through the side door. Martha could hear someone else, Andrew probably, unsealing the door at the front. They were ready to leave. They must have looked into her room and found it dark and decided that she had slipped away, as John had, without good-byes.

One car, and then another and a third—taxis—had driven up the boardwalk to reach the front door. She could hear voices, instructions to the drivers. Matthew called, "To the airport!" and that vibrant sound carried over the night air and through the closed kitchen door.

Martha sat at the table and looked at the turkey. By her elbow was the wine she had offered to Thaddaeus. It hardly filled a glass, and it was sour and gritty with sediment. Absently she dug into the turkey for a forkful of her breadcrumb dressing. She found it soggy and too heavily spiced with chestnut. Even so, she emptied the glass and licked the prongs of her fork.